A Small-Town Marriage

》》》》》》》》》》　《《《《《《《《《《《

The Marchesa Colombi

A Small-Town Marriage

TRANSLATED FROM THE ITALIAN
AND WITH AN AFTERWORD
BY PAULA SPURLIN PAIGE

NORTHWESTERN UNIVERSITY PRESS
EVANSTON, ILLINOIS

》》》》》》》》》》》　《《《《《《《《《《《

Northwestern University Press
Evanston, Illinois 60208-4210

English translation and translator's afterword
copyright © 2001 by Northwestern University Press.
Published 2001. All rights reserved.

First published in Italian in 1885 by Galli as *Un matrimonio in provincia*.

Printed in the United States of America

10 9 8 7 6 5 4 3 2

ISBN 0-8101-1841-6

Library of Congress Cataloging-in-Publication Data

Colombi, Marchesa, 1840–1920.
    [Matrimonio in provincia. English]
    A small-town marriage / the Marchesa Colombi ; translated from the
Italian and with an afterword by Paula Spurlin Paige.
        p.   cm.
    Includes bibliographical references.
    ISBN 0-8101-1841-6 (alk. paper)
    I. Paige, Paula Spurlin. II. Title.
    PQ4733.T7 M313 2001
    853'.8—dc21

                                                                    2001000944

》》》 CONTENTS 《《《

A Small-Town Marriage

It would be difficult to imagine a drearier childhood, or one more monotonous and joyless than mine. When I think back on it, after so many, many years, I can still feel the endless gloom of that dead calm going on and on, unchanging, all through the long stretches of time that separated the few events that took place in our family life.

I never knew my mother, who died during the first year of my life. Our family consisted of my father, the notary Pietro Dellara; of his old aunt, a little old spinster as dried up as a herring, who slept in the kitchen where, in order to hide her bed, she had put up a screen behind which she spent her life in the dark; of my elder sister Caterina, called Titina; and of me, who had inherited from my godfather the unfortunate name of Gaudenzia, which my family had shortened to the ridiculous diminutive "Denza."

We had a house . . . heavens, what a house! There was an entrance room of normal size, but so bright that it dazzled the eyes, and it was absolutely devoid of furniture. There was not even a place to leave your hat. The room was cluttered with flowerpots containing bits of dry soil, and some stumps of plants that had died of thirst because no one had bothered to water them; when necessary they were used to prop open the living-room door.

The vast, square living room—bright, too bright, because it had no curtains or hangings or sheers on the windows—was furnished with a sofa against the main wall opposite the windows, four armchairs—two to the right and two to the left of the sofa, pushed up against the wall—and eight chairs along the side walls, four on each side. In the center of the room was a round table covered with a wool throw; and on the rosette in the middle of the throw was a glove box with a glass lid, through which you could see a pair of slightly worn white gloves. The box was a wedding gift from my father to his bride, and the gloves were the ones that my poor mother had worn on her wedding day. Around the box, lined up precisely on the table, were two napkin rings embroidered on canvas with the words BUON APPETITO, a cigar case of red velvet with a pansy embroidered in silk, and a case made of dark leather lined with turquoise satin, which was always left open to show a rattle and a little silver plate that my godfather Gaudenzio had given my mother when I was born.

None of these objects had ever been used for its intended purpose, because my father thought them too luxurious for everyday use and consequently kept them in the living room, which was the luxurious room of the house.

After the living room came Papa's bedroom, with a big double bed that took up the whole room. At the head of the bed were two holy water basins made of engraved silver, which had become more beautiful as they had tarnished with time, two more porcelain basins shaped like angels with skirts raised to form a goblet, and, finally, a fifth brass basin that, even though it had lost its silver, was the only one that actually contained holy water. Over the basins hung lots of olive and palm branches, and a bundle of votive candles from which you could count the years that had passed since Papa's marriage, beginning with the first years—symbolized by little fragments of candles held together only by their cotton wicks, on which these old pieces of blackened wax dangled like a string of sausages—and passing gradually, year by year, to candles that were encrusted, crumbling and twisted, then to some that were still whole but that ran the gamut of griminess (going from brown through every shade of yellow, down to last year's, still intact, almost white, with little red- and green-painted flowers, which were quite lovely).

To the right of the bed was a strongbox, where Papa kept his money and what he called "the family relics" compulsively locked up: daguerreotype portraits of him and my mother as newlyweds, which had almost completely faded away; the little bonnet that we had worn at our baptisms; a pile of yellowed sheets of paper containing my father's youthful poetic efforts; and, finally, my mother's jewels.

On the other side of the big bed there were eight high-backed chairs, but they were neither antique nor beautiful, just old, and they were lined up like so many soldiers. And if by chance one of them got moved out the slightest bit from the wall or got turned a hair toward the one next to it, Papa hastened to put it back in place, and was not happy until he had made sure—by bending and taking aim as though he was going to fire a shot—that the eight chairs formed a flawless straight line.

After Papa's room there was an enormous kitchen, where our aunt had staked out her bedroom with the screen; this still left plenty of room for an ordinary kitchen table and a larger walnut table where we had our meals.

In back of the kitchen there was a large low-ceilinged room with whitewashed walls where Titina and I slept. Our beds were the primitive kind, made of trestles and benches topped with a bed-sack and a mattress. And at the head of the bed we also had a basin of holy water, but ours was made of fired clay like the kitchen pots; sacred pictures that were pasted to the wall for want of frames; and a hazelnut rosary with a nut for every Our Father (this last item had made us commit countless sins of gluttony in our hearts and owed its salvation early on to its sacred nature, and later to its rancid stench).

There was no garden, or courtyard, or balcony where we could go for a breath of fresh air. In recompense, however, our father had a passion—or rather a mania—for exercise. For all illnesses, for every problem that life posed, he admitted only two remedies, but they were infallible: lighting a lamp to the Madonna and exercising.

He also used them preventively, as simple hygienic measures, because in our house we didn't have illnesses or problems; and yet we went to light the lamp every Friday, and, as for exercising, the soles of my feet still hurt when I think of it.

Heavens! How we walked on those wide straight main roads, white with snow in the winter and with dust in the summer, which stretched out as far as the eye could see over the vast plains, among the meadows and rice fields of the lower Novarese region!

I have said that Papa was a notary, but his office was not exactly besieged by clients. He kept a young apprentice and was able to take care of everything with his help, and he still had time left over for our horrendous walks.

In the morning he made us get up very early, hardly giving us enough time to get dressed; then we were off: leaving the house in a mess, the beds unmade, we went back and forth along any main road, any one, it didn't matter, with no destination.

To him it didn't matter whether or not the scenery was beautiful; he didn't aspire to mountain treks or anything like that. His only passion was to put one foot in front of the other, for so many hours in a row, and to be able to say when we came back: "We did so many kilometers."

When we came home we were tired, and we didn't feel up to the drudgery of housework. There was a servant who came in at eight in the morning and left around two. In that time she had to put the house in order, go to market, cook, wait on table, and clean up afterward.

Consequently, everything was done in a very perfunctory way. But Papa was always happy with anything he was given to eat and, as for housekeeping, he only cared if the furniture was in its proper place and the chairs were neatly lined up; and, as long as we exercised, he asked no more.

He didn't even send us to school, because he said that all those hours of immobility were deadly. From time to time he taught us to read and write and to do arithmetic. And during our walks, he took care of our literary education.

Or so he thought, because he would recite to us from the *Iliad,* the *Aeneid,* and *Jerusalem Delivered.* He would grow animated and gesture as he told of heroes fighting alone against armies, picking up boulders as big as mountains and throwing them at the enemy, performing the most stupefying, amazing feats; and, when he finished his stories, poor Papa would be puffing and sweating, as though he were the one who had done these deeds.

We certainly did not share his admiration. Deprived of the beauty of their form, tossed off like this between a couple of cornfields, these stories struck us as extravagant, and we failed to see how they could constitute our literary education. We confused them with some outlandish tales that our aunt used to tell us on rainy evenings and didn't even find them any more worthwhile.

Between lunch and supper we took another walk on another main road, or perhaps on the same one we had taken in the morning.

At supper we ate leftovers from lunch cold, and then we went out again; we would race from one side of Novara to the market, a big four-sided building surrounded on all sides by handsome, tall, spacious porticos, and we would go round and round that building, beneath those deserted, echoing arcades, until we were satisfied that we had done a sufficient number of kilometers to be able to go to bed with a quiet conscience.

We were not unhappy with this regimen, and we certainly were not bored. But neither were we happy, and we didn't have any fun. What we felt was apathy, total indifference.

In the fall some distant relatives of ours whom we referred to as cousins came home from boarding school, and before they left for the country Papa would take us to visit them. They had a living room that was not much better than ours, but since they spent much of their time in it, had flowers, and rearranged the furniture, it seemed a completely different place.

They entertained us there, among their embroidery and their books; they would greet us graciously and informally and would shake hands with Papa, saying with a courage that we found quite terrifying, "Good morning, sir."

Then they turned to us very politely and asked, "Would you like to go play in the other room, or would you prefer to stay here and talk?"

For us both things were equally impossible. We had never played. No one had ever given us a toy or a doll, and there was no room for running or jumping in our house. Our only recreation was those endless walks. And when torrential rains or a three-foot snowfall or a heat wave of ninety-five degrees in the shade—some act of God—made our walks impossible for a few days, we were supposed to spend those hours learning the famous three R's.

The result was that we knew neither how to play nor how to converse; so when our Bonelli cousins asked that question we looked at each other in confusion and didn't answer.

So they would say, "Well, let's stay here and talk."

They would move a small bench in front of the window and pull up four very low little armchairs; then they would sit down and have us sit down, and the four of us would put up our feet on the same bench "in order to be closer," they said, as though we were very intimate. But whether we were close together or not, we never knew what to say. However, they were so nice and charming, and they knew so many things, that we were happy just to look at them, and to listen to them chatting about the boarding school where they had been, and about the countryside where they were going.

Then when they returned from the country, they would come to see us before they went back to boarding school and, if they managed to find us at home, which wasn't easy, we would receive them majestically in the living room, saying, "Please sit down," and finally we would sit down ourselves on the sofa, by way of example. And they would say, "Oh, thank you, thank you," but they would never sit down and would flit around, touching everything on the table, the glove box, the napkin rings, the goblet, asking every time who had made this or given us that; and we would repeat the story of each object.

Then Papa, whom we had called to help us, would hurry into the room, and somehow after a few minutes he would be narrating, melodramatically and with flourishing gestures, some heroic deeds wrought by the two Ajaxes, or some angry fit of Orlando's. And the girls would laugh and understand and prompt Papa, because they, too, knew the names of the heroes of those poems of Papa's, as though they were personal friends.

Titina would say, "That's because they've already completed their literary education."

Afterward, for the rest of the year, we would talk over those visits, just the two of us, or with our aunt. Auntie would listen to us with a big silly smile that showed all the cavities in her false teeth; she seemed to delight in our chatter and tried to participate in the conversation, too. But when she laughed, she never managed to understand why something was funny, and she would laugh for some completely different reason.

Once the Bonellis had told us that old saw about a lady who looked at the train schedule to see where she might take a trip; seeing "Novara, Trecate, Magenta, Milan, and vice versa," she said, "Let's go to Vice Versa!"

This made us laugh for a whole year; and the following year we thought that we would go on laughing about it with our cousins, but they had forgotten it; when we brought it up they barely managed a smile, saying that it was "old nonsense."

But when our hilarity was at its height, Auntie made us tell the story many times; then she broke out into loud, convulsive laughter, exclaiming "The Vice's verses! The Vice's verses!" while she did a pantomime of someone scribbling poetry.

In our parish there was a vicar whom she and her pious friends called the Vice, whom they fussed over and talked about continuously. So she thought that the story contained a pointless reference to her "Vice," and it was impossible to disabuse her of that idea, which she found enormously amusing.

Besides, she had little time to chat. She suffered from rheumatism and was constantly busy putting on or taking off a layer of flannel as soon as the temperature went up or down a degree.

Moreover, she had her church services, which took up much of her morning. Then there was the servant, whom she fancied she was teaching to cook—an art that was completely foreign to her and for which she demonstrated a phenomenal lack of aptitude.

∽

These are the memories of my childhood, the age of smiles, of pleasures, of all those wonderful things that people talk and write about.

Then came my youth.

Between youth and childhood, however, when I was hardly more than fourteen, the first big event of our family life took place.

Papa married an old lady, whom we had known for quite a while, and of whom we were completely in awe. For years and years we had seen her come to church in the winter completely enveloped in a big violet flannel coat, with a shawl over her arm to cover her legs when she sat down, because her knees got cold. She wore a bizarre hat with a long silk collar that hung down her back, to protect her neck from drafts. She always kept a brass ball full of hot water in her muff, and she constantly chewed on a piece of star anise to help her digestion. She had had the top of her head shaved, because her hair was very thin, and she hoped that it would grow in thicker. But it had not grown back at all, and she always wore a wig over the shaved part.

We thought that she was fifty, our aunt's age, which for us was the height of antiquity. We later learned that she was forty-three, but it was all the same to us.

Imagine our hilarity when we heard that Papa was getting married! He told us, "You understand, my dears, that I am acting in your interest. My estate is very, very small: I don't make much from my practice; your mother's dowry has dwindled to ten thousand lire. This good lady has sixty thousand lire, which will eventually be yours, because she has no relatives, and she loves me. . . . Besides, she will look after you, now that you are older and need the kind of help that Auntie can't give you."

Nonetheless, those were wonderful times, during their engagement and the wedding.

It was autumn. Our cousins were home from boarding school, and it seemed incredible to visit them bearing such exciting news. In fact, we had barely sat down, with our eight feet propped on the bench, when they said to us, "So, there's to be a bride in your house, is there?" And they began to laugh, and so did we, only more so. Really, what a farce! We calculated that, if we added up all four of our ages, the total would barely equal the bride's. Giuseppina, the eldest cousin, who was fifteen, said haughtily, "And after we get this bride married off, we'll have to think about finding a husband for Auntie!"

Oh, what fun we had! Papa's fiancée had the four of us come every day to her house, where, on the day of her engagement, she had set on the living-room table a big tray of sugared almonds so that we could help ourselves. And things went on like this until the day they were married, for a month and a half or two months.

What fun! We would all gather around the tray and make all kinds of nasty, silly jokes at the bride's expense while we polished off the almonds: "How lovely she'll be dressed in white! How charming she will be when she says *tu* to her groom, looking so young. She'll stick orange blossoms in her wig."

And this kind of nonsense amused us as though it were the height of wit!

After the wedding the couple went away, and we stayed alone for a week with our aunt, who let us go out only in the early morning to go to church. But we still had the wedding almonds, and the gifts, and the time passed quickly.

Then one evening Papa came back with his wife, who was now healthy and strong; she had stopped chewing on star anise and she was eating cornmeal, beans, and cucumbers and every kind of indigestible food, and she walked like a mailman. . . . In short, that week of travel and her "change of situation," as she called it, had made a new woman of her. She was full of life and animation.

She had all her own parlor furniture moved into our living room. By coincidence, it was exactly the same as ours: a sofa, eight chairs, four armchairs, and a round table. Only ours were green and the bride's were red! There was no way to arrange them together; the two colors clashed terribly.

The bride solved the problem by putting the red furniture against the right wall, and the green against the left wall, each with its respective table in front of it, as though it were a separate arrangement. The main wall—the one opposite the windows—became a neutral ground, in which the two living-room sets each advanced from its own side, nearly up to the halfway point; then they stopped at a theoretical line of demarcation, which indicated the space to be left between the last red chair and the first green one.

And the visits began.

They were great fun for us. We would run into the living room and sit openmouthed to hear what was being said. Even Auntie, carried away by this new state of affairs, put on a dress that was softer, blacker, and more clinging than usual and a dazzling white bonnet with a pretty starched frill that framed her face and came to sit in the living room, smiling quietly with her hands folded in her lap.

The new bride waited until the guests had left then told us quite nonchalantly, "Next time there's no need for you girls to come to the living room when there are guests. As for you, Auntie, I don't need any help: that's the only advantage of marrying late in life."

So Auntie went quietly back behind her screen, and we went back to our lonely room.

The walks on the main road began again, in the company of the bride, who leaned triumphantly on Papa's arm and told us to go on ahead. But we were excluded from the evening stroll around the arcade. The only time when we had ever seen any civilized, well-dressed people was in fact when we crossed the city after supper on our way to the market arcade. Farewell to all that! Never again.

When the first months of the honeymoon were over, our step-mother turned her attention to the household and found that it was in great disarray. This was true. She realized that we knew nothing about cooking, which was also true. She declared that it was stupid to spend money to eat Auntie's sauces. A third undeniable truth.

And she made this pronouncement: "You learn nothing by running about on the main roads." Papa modestly observed that he "recited from the classics" while we were walking, but she shrugged and said, "Yes, I understand, but they can manage just as well without all that. I don't even know what the classics are, and I found a husband just the same. A little late," she added, with that unflappable candor that kept you from making fun of her, "but after all, I did find one. So, you don't learn anything by running around all day. They already know enough about 'reading, writing, and arithmetic'; girls don't have to be professors. Now's the time for them to learn to keep a house in order, to sew, iron, cook, and be good housewives."

No one could find fault with these words of wisdom: therefore even the long walks on the main roads, white with snow or dust, were given up, and we embarked on a completely different life.

Our stepmother bought two small straw chairs, which she arranged on either side of the kitchen window, between the little table and Auntie's screen, and she had Titina and me sit facing each other with a wicker basket between us, full of laundry to be mended.

In the morning she made us sweep, dust, and make the beds; we bustled through the house covered with big canvas aprons; then she sent us to our rooms to dress and do our hair. And when we were presentable, we had to sit and do needlework. But when it was time to make dinner, as we each had to do for a week, we left our needlework and learned to cook under our stepmother's supervision, which was more able and energetic than Auntie's had been.

Even if we had tried, we couldn't really have said, in all good conscience, that she did us any harm. If only she had tempered her instruction and her ordering us about with a bit of kindness! But this was not in her character, or in the sound of her voice, or in her mannerisms. She was sharp by nature, and to her sharpness meant sincerity. In fact, she was sincere, and she would say whatever she thought frankly. She didn't understand politeness; to her it was affectation.

We had been badly brought up, by a man and an old woman. We weren't used to discipline and work. That year we began to feel unhappy with our life.

The next year was much worse. They had a son, and, even though he was sent out to board with a nurse in Trecate, he became the king of the household. Our stepmother refused the gift of a dress that Papa wanted her to pick out and told him to give her the same amount of cash instead, and she would put it in a savings account "for her heir."

A short while later she said that since she was old and didn't live a fancy life, she had no need for jewels, and it was a sin to keep capital tied up in earrings and brooches.

So she sold all the jewelry that had been given to her personally and used the money to buy a field next to a parcel of land that she already owned, "for her heir."

One of the many other economy measures that she came up with was to have most of the corn that was raised on Papa's farmlands ground, and to have the family eat a lot of cornmeal. One day a cart arrived loaded with innumerable sacks of flour, which were stacked in the foyer and even in the living room, our elegant room.

"They only take up one corner," she would say. "You can hardly see them. . . ." But a short while later came the supplies of potatoes, chestnuts, apples, and rice; and all this food piled up in the living room, which turned into a sort of storeroom. Papa pointed out that we no longer had any place to entertain.

But our stepmother had a ready answer.

"To entertain whom? You mean my visitors? Because people who want to speak with you come to your office downstairs. Well, my visitors will find a sofa and armchairs, which is what a living room is supposed to contain. The food supplies are something extra, which convey an impression of abundance that can hardly fail to please any serious person. Moreover, visits are not a necessity of life, and since I hardly visit anyone myself, people will end up not visiting me. Flour, potatoes, and fruit, on the other hand, are family necessities."

She was always right. In fact, most of the visitors stopped coming. Our few relatives, who stopped by rather infrequently, were received in Papa's bedroom, now the master bedroom, where there was always a fire burning in the fireplace. So the living room acquired a layer of dust under the old sheets covering the furniture and was transformed definitively into a storeroom. Which was a perfect use for it, since it had neither a fireplace nor a heater, and was as cold as a cellar. The potatoes froze.

Meanwhile, I had turned sixteen. I had grown quite tall and had filled out proportionately. My clothes were always tearing at the waist or bursting at the seams around the armholes or in back, and buttons were always popping off and buttonholes fraying: it was enough to drive one mad.

Moreover, I still wore my hair off my forehead, pulled back and gathered on the neck in a thick knot, like a schoolgirl, and short skirts just down to the ankle that exposed my entire foot, which was neither small nor pretty; my feet were encased in big, solidly made shoes designed to accommodate the extraordinary amount of exercise that Papa considered a necessity of life.

When our stepmother's child was barely six months old, his wet-nurse got sick and we had to bring him home and raise him on formula.

When I held the brat in my arms—I was the one who had to lug him around the house all day, because Titina wasn't strong enough to carry him for very long—my stepmother would look at me approvingly and say, "Those arms were just made to hold a child! Doesn't she look like a beautiful bride from Trecate or Oleggio, with her first little boy?"

I didn't find her words the least bit flattering, because, in fact, with my blooming looks and skimpy clothes I looked like a peasant from one or another of those villages, and this was mortifying. Once I tried to tell her this.

"You know, with these short dresses and my hair like this I look like a farmgirl. I should part my hair over my forehead, and bring it down over my ears, and lengthen my skirts just a bit, enough to cover my feet. . . ."

But my stepmother exclaimed, "What next? What's got into you? With that face of yours, pale as a moon, and those big eyes shining like two lanterns, people look at you more than they should as it is, and you overshadow your poor sister, for heaven's sake! On top of that, if we dress you like a woman who's looking for a husband, it's all over for Titina. She'll never get married."

As a matter of fact, Titina *was* a bit of a wallflower compared to me. She was small and blond and pretty, with light eyes and no eyelashes, and she looked like a wax doll.

The possibility of hurting her chances kept me from insisting that I dress like a proper young woman. But when I had to go out walking in a getup like that, with the baby hanging around my neck, in front of Papa and my stepmother, I would get so angry that I don't know why I didn't just waste away from aggravation.

On top of all that, everybody would look at me and smile, and whisper among themselves.

Once, when we came home after one of those awful walks, Titina said, giving me a look of astonishment, "Do you know that you're beautiful, Denza?"

Embarrassed, I repeated, "Beautiful . . . ?"

But I must admit that I was a bit less stupefied than my sister. I had often overheard snatches of the observations uttered by the men who watched me in the street: "A handsome young woman . . . ," "Beautiful face . . . ," "Lovely big eyes . . . ," "Fresh as a rose. . . ."

And every time, when I got home, I had gone to the mirror to see whether they were telling the truth.

And sweet Titina—thunderstruck at the idea that the magic quality that she thought belonged only to the heroines of Papa's fairytales and poems could be found right here at home, under my humble rags—went on, "Yes, indeed, Denza. I heard a man who stopped to look at you say, 'What a lovely girl! She's a beauty!'"

We were having this conversation in our bedroom. Our step-mother overheard us from the kitchen and, with her usual abrupt frankness, opened the door, stuck her head in, and said, "A beauty, no, because she's a little too blooming and rustic looking for that, but she *is* beautiful. And that's just why—because she's beautiful and you're not, and because you're the eldest—I don't want to dress her in frills. If I do, she'll find a husband in a week, and I'll still be saddled with you—which you would probably like even less than I do. I don't fuss and fawn over you, but I do look out for your interests, just as though I were your mother, and one day you'll thank me for it. And now, into the kitchen! And take care not to let this beauty notion go to your head! Even if you are beautiful, you've done nothing to deserve it, and it won't make you a better person, or more fortunate, or more loved than anyone else. Look at me: I'm ugly, and old to boot, and I've found the best husband in the world; there are few wives who are more loved than I am."

In spite of their sharpness, these words caused me great joy, and filled me with a feeling of rapture, as though I had acquired a treasure, a real reason to be happy.

Her warning not to let my beauty go to my head had quite the opposite effect. It did go straight to my head, and now I thought of nothing else, except how wonderful it was to be beautiful. The fact that this didn't make me a better person, or luckier, or more lovable did not matter in the slightest to me. It certainly did make people admire me, and that was what gave me pleasure.

I eventually adopted a certain contemptuous air when I went out so badly dressed, as though to express what I really thought: Here I am. Even in a getup like this I'm beautiful. I don't need frills to be admired!

However, after a while I grew bored with this transient admiration from people whom I didn't know, or at least it lost its excitement. I became impatient for Titina to get married, so that I could dress like other girls my age. I was almost seventeen: I couldn't spend my entire life with my feet sticking out beneath my skirt and my hair fixed like a schoolgirl's just because my sister wasn't married. Besides, my stepmother had said that if I were properly dressed I would find a husband in a week. And now, because I had to live in that ugly house, with its thrifty, hardworking ways, and be saddled with that tiresome brat with his little old man's face that showed his parents' age, I was dying to get married.

Until now I had always slept blissfully through the long nights: I went to bed as soon as they sent me to my room, often without even lighting the candle, drowsily exchanging a few words with Titina as I undressed, and I would fall asleep as soon as I hit the sheets, and sleep the sleep of a plump, healthy wench.

After my stepmother's memorable words about beauty, however, it became impossible for me to go to bed in the dark. I would light the candle, and take down my hair in front of a tiny mirror a couple of inches square, the only concession to vanity among the furniture in our room, which we hadn't had much use for until now.

Titina couldn't get over the change in me. She always asked, "But why are you taking your hair down? You know you just have to braid it again when you go to bed. . . ."

Once she asked me, laughing as though it were the strangest idea, "Is it because people have told you how pretty you are that you've started to undo your hair in front of the mirror?"

I turned quite red and answered that she was being silly, that it didn't make the slightest difference to me whether I was beautiful or ugly. But I had never told a lie before; Papa had raised us with a reverence for truth, and my honest heart was heavy with that first untruth. I felt as though I had a great sin on my conscience. That sentence from the Christian catechism that says "You must not tell a lie even to save the entire world" was ringing in my ears.

I had studied catechism to prepare for my First Communion and, although I had not done so with any particular religious fervor, I had accepted its dogma quite literally, convinced that, since it was written down and everybody believed it—at least, I didn't know anyone who didn't believe it—it must be true. And I had never doubted it for an instant. It had never even occurred to me that it was possible to doubt it.

And now I found myself telling a lie: I had committed that terrible sin that should not be committed even to save the entire world, and I had done so under no such extenuating circumstances, not having even one tiny bit of the world to save.

I sighed loudly as I tossed and turned in my bed, so that Titina kept waking up just as she fell asleep. Finally she overcame her sleepy torpor and murmured, "What's the matter? Why are you sighing like that?"

Anxious to remove that weight from my conscience, I answered in a tragic voice, "I've told a lie: that's what's the matter. . . ."

I hoped that Titina would ask me questions, so that I could get up my courage to tell her everything. But she only muttered sleepily, "Oh, you'll go to confession. . . ." And she turned to the wall, getting into a comfortable position again so that she could sleep in peace.

In fact, the idea of confession was comforting. Why hadn't it occurred to me that sins were wiped away by absolution? True, there's purgatory, but I couldn't conceive of anything so remote.

So having decided to confess everything at some future time and get a blanket absolution, I gave myself up to the guilty joy of thinking myself beautiful, and that, among the many who said so and then disappeared, there would be one who would not disappear, who would follow me home at a distance, and who would then enter Papa's study and ask for my hand.

My stepmother had said that if I were properly dressed this would happen in a week. So I calculated that, since I was badly dressed, it would take another week, or maybe two, or a month, at the most. All things considered, however, it had to happen, because it was obvious that anyone could tell that I was beautiful in spite of my awful, ridiculous clothes. I knew it, because I heard it so often.

What would that young man be like?

I couldn't imagine his face. But it stirred me to think about him, and I loved him. This nameless, formless figure, who remained vague even in my imagination, was my most precious thought.

I thought that he would hold me tight, and give me a feeling of affectionate warmth, which I ardently desired and which I felt so lacking in my life, because no one had ever hugged me, not even Papa, since I was little. And he would whisper to me, "Dearest . . . how lovely you are!"

I couldn't imagine anything in detail: the wedding, the honeymoon, my wardrobe, or house. . . . No, all that would flash by in a moment, in fits and starts, only to vanish. The only scene that I could clearly imagine, which recurred with the persistence of an obsession and of which I never tired, was a young man embracing me tightly and murmuring, "Dearest . . . how lovely you are!"

The next morning, while we were each dressing on opposite sides of the bed, Titina said, "What was the matter last night, with that talk about a lie? Were you dreaming?"

I got up my courage and answered, convinced that I was doing something admirable, "No, I wasn't dreaming. I told you that it doesn't matter to me whether I'm pretty or ugly, but it's not true. . . . It does matter a great deal to me, and I'm glad I'm pretty, and that's why I take down my hair in front of the mirror, just as you thought. There!"

I said "There!" with a big sigh, as though to say, *Now I've made amends.* And I felt lighter, satisfied with myself; but I didn't dare look at Titina.

She seemed a bit shaken. This conversation, and my confession, were beyond the scope of our usual exchanges. Disconcerted, she looked at me hesitantly, then forced a smile and said with a shrug, "Now you're starting to make scenes. . . . You really are crazy!"

And she didn't refer to it again.

∽

One day our cousins the Bonellis, who had finished boarding school and were living the life of very elegant young ladies, invited us to go with them to the opera, where they were putting on *Faust*. And our stepmother agreed that we could go, "since it didn't cost anything."

We wore light wool summer dresses with a white background scattered with green leaves; and, since it was winter and we were used to wearing dark clothes, we thought we were quite elegant in our light-colored dresses.

When we entered the box at the theater, there were our cousins dressed in white, in full evening dress, with flowers in their hair, and this took us down a peg.

We changed seats between each act so that we could each sit for a while at the railing that ran along two sides of the box, where we could see and be seen better. It was an elegant box, with a long thin mirror embedded in the white stucco and gold-traced doors. When it was my cousin Maria's and my turn to move forward—Giuseppina and Titina got to go first because they were the eldest—I saw myself reflected in the mirror behind Maria, who was across from me, and I almost didn't recognize myself: so dazzling was that white face, with its rosy cheeks and shining eyes, transformed by the fun and excitement of the occasion. It was more interesting to me than what was happening on stage, which I didn't understand much of and found intimidating, because it was the first time I had ever seen an opera.

Maria, who went more often, tried to explain the story to me. She said, "That handsome young man there is the old man from the first act. And the other one, with the skinny legs, is the devil who has made him young again, in exchange for his soul. Now it gets really good. As soon as Faust becomes young, he falls in love with Marguerite."

Then the performance really began to interest me. How did he fall in love? Oh, how eagerly I waited for that moment! When Faust bent amorously toward Marguerite, murmuring sweet nothings to her in the softest of voices, I felt as though I were consumed with love, just as though he had murmured these things to me. I would have liked to know what he said to her, but they were singing, and the music drowned out the words. I didn't understand much of the plot, but the love scenes remained engraved in my mind.

As we were walking home—quickly, because it was freezing out, and in Novara there weren't any carriages to rent on the street— Maria took my arm and said, "Well, my beauty, you know that you've made a conquest, don't you?"

"Have I? Who?"

It should be noted that I had never heard that expression "make a conquest"; it wasn't part of our household vocabulary. And yet I understood it intuitively, by coquettish instinct, as though I had been familiar with it for some time.

Maria answered, "Oh, come on! Do you mean that you didn't notice?"

I protested, with a forthrightness born of ignorance, "No, really . . . you know, I was having such a good time looking at myself in that long mirror behind you that I didn't see anyone."

Maria burst out laughing, and said, "You vain thing! And you even admit it so openly? Aren't you ashamed of being so vain?"

I reflected for a moment, and then I answered very frankly, so as not to tell another lie, "No, *you* say that I'm a beauty. You're the ones who say it, and I just look at myself. But who is my conquest? Tell me!"

"Mazzucchetti. You know, the son of those old landowners who live out toward Sant' Eufemia. He's an only child, and very rich. He watched you all evening through his opera glasses."

"Oh, what a shame that I didn't see him! What's he like? Is he handsome?"

"Yes . . . well, he's . . . he's . . . he's a bit fat. But if you look closely he's got nice features. He's a good-looking young man. And he's undergoing treatment for his weight problem. His parents spare no expense when it comes to him, even though they're miserly. Last summer they took him to Monsummano in Tuscany to take steam baths, to make him sweat out the fat, you know. Then they took him up to Oropa, which is I don't know how many meters above sea level, so that the cold would make him lose weight, and hydropathy . . ."

I was quite taken aback by the idea of such obesity, and I said, "But he must be a whale! And is he any thinner now?"

"Yes . . . yes, a bit . . . but no matter: fat or thin, he's a wonderful match. His mother had a dowry of two hundred thousand lire, and his father must have twice that."

I was astonished! How much that girl knew! Spa towns and which provinces they were in, the effects of cures, the value of family fortunes . . . she had it all on the tip of her tongue. How was it possible that anyone could be interested in me, when there were girls like her around?

We had reached their door, and our cousins said goodnight. We went on with Papa, and I didn't say another word the rest of the way home.

My heart brimmed over with affection for Maria. I felt a need to express it, and so as soon as I was alone with Titina I burst out, "How lovely Maria looked tonight!"

Titina answered indifferently, as she turned down the blankets on her bed, "Giuseppina looked lovelier."

In fact, Giuseppina was lovelier. But she had never told me of anyone's falling in love with me. She had never cared about my looks, except to complain that my clothes made me look terrible. Besides, she was more beautiful than I was, slimmer and taller; she was an elegant figure of a woman, and she didn't admire me in the slightest. I could not adore her as I did her sister, who could forget herself and worry about me, and *who had found me* a lover. I sincerely felt that I owed this to her; I was immensely grateful, and I wanted to express it. So I said to my sister, "I prefer Maria. She's always been my favorite—my friend!"

Titina shook her head with a knowing smile, and repeated that phrase that she often said to me, "You really are crazy! Since when is Maria your friend? We see each other so seldom. . . ."

"No, now that she's finished school, we see each other more often."

"Less rarely, you mean. But at any rate, there hasn't been time for any great friendship."

"Friendship doesn't take a lot of time. It's a feeling of attraction. . . ."

Titina laughed again, and asked somewhat ironically, "Where did you read that?"

I shrugged, murmuring, "Idiot!"

I had no real reason to be angry. My sister was in a snit that evening, the poor soul! Perhaps she had noticed that nobody looked at her at the theater, because I overshadowed her and drew attention away from her. . . . After all, she was eighteen! But perhaps she was also jealous of my sudden infatuation with Maria, since she had been my only friend and confidante until now. Looking at the ceiling, she said in a different voice, "I read somewhere that you know who your real friends are when you're unhappy. Were you unhappy tonight?"

"No!" I burst out, with a spontaneous cry of joy. "I was happy, so happy! You know who your friends are when you're happy!"

These words offended my sister, and I knew it. Perhaps she was right: all of our past life together, a life of kindness, docility, and resignation, was less important to me than a few flattering words from an elegant little chatterbox. However, at the time I did not think that Titina was in the right, and I went to bed without another word.

From that evening on I began to live with my mind far removed from the household and my everyday tasks. And having a new focus in my life, so different from the thoughts that had absorbed me until then, did wonders to dispel the gloom of that house and to lighten the burden of my chores.

I would put the baby to sleep, get him dressed when he woke up, and cook—all through sheer mechanical force of habit, without noticing what I did, without letting my attention wander from the sweet reverie that absorbed my entire being.

All that was important to me was to see that young man, and, consequently, it was important that I see Maria again. I had to go out with her so that she could point him out to me when we ran into him.

I began to make amazingly daring proposals. I suggested to Papa and to my stepmother that we owed the Bonellis a visit, to thank them for the evening at the opera.

My stepmother answered that this wasn't at all pressing. So I told them how much I liked the Church of Sant' Eufemia, and that I would like to go to mass there the following Sunday.

This did not go down well, either. My stepmother shook her head disapprovingly and said, "It seems as though you concoct these odd schemes on purpose, just like those spoiled girls who expect their parents to satisfy their slightest whim. You do know, though, that I will never do you any harm or deprive you of anything that you need—but I will not put up with whims on any account. San Gaudenzio is right here, and then both San Marco and the Duomo are close by. . . ."

I had expected not only a refusal but also that series of observations that always accompanied my stepmother's answers, whether affirmative or negative. But Maria had told me that the Mazzucchettis lived near Sant' Eufemia, and so intense was the hope of seeing my suitor that I was led to make this desperate attempt.

On the street I looked attentively at all the plump men, and it seemed to me that I had always hated thin ones. However, I only looked at the plump men who were young and elegant.

Finally we did go to visit our cousins. I smiled to myself as I climbed the stairs, thinking that Maria would speak of him as soon as she saw me. I shook her hand hard, blushing, not daring to look at her. I counted on her tact to find a way of taking me aside to talk without anyone overhearing.

But she seemed to have other things on her mind.

Our stepmother had stopped in Signor Bonelli's office, and the four of us, along with the brat, were standing together near a window in the living room. They were talking about the masked balls at the end of Carnival, and about a dance that Giuseppina and Maria had attended. Maria was describing what they had worn that evening: white crepe trimmed with pale roses, and the top, instead of being décolleté, buttoned on one side, instead of the usual way in the middle.

Titina listened with rapt attention, and asked for explanations. What side did the top button on? On the right or on the left? And were the buttons only on one side, in some unusual way, or on both sides, so that they met in the middle?

I was beginning to shiver: time was passing, and I expected our stepmother to say at any moment that it was time for us to go. Why didn't Maria speak about what was on my mind? Perhaps she was being overcautious. But I was so fixated on that idea that I wanted her to talk about it even with our sisters present, rather than not talk about it at all.

In fact, I finally wanted Titina to know "everything." I could not keep her ignorant of such an important fact in my life. Besides, I needed someone to confide in at home, on our walks, in our room, during the day, at night, anytime. . . . I saw Maria all too seldom.

I thought of asking who was at the party, thinking that Maria would take advantage of the opportunity to mention him and tell me something about him, more or less openly.

It was Giuseppina who answered, enumerating the married and unmarried women at length. I let her finish, then asked again, "And who were the men there?"

"Men . . . let's see. So-and-so, and that other man, the two X brothers, Captain Somebody . . ." And she went on like this for quite a while, with Maria adding a name from time to time. Titina was showing obvious signs of boredom, because we didn't know any of these people, either personally or by name. I, on the other hand, was trembling; I felt myself growing pale, and my heart was pounding hard. Finally Giuseppina said, "And there was Mazzucchetti, with his three friends. . . ."

I looked hard at Maria, waiting eagerly, but she was intent on remembering who was there, and she mentioned two or three others, without taking any particular notice of Mazzucchetti's name, as though she hadn't heard it.

Losing my temper, I shifted the child, who was dozing on my chest, from one arm to the other and told them to stop that litany of names, that we didn't know any of them, and that it was no fun for me to go on talking with that brat on my hands; that I couldn't get rid of him for a single minute; that I was fed up with washing him, and dressing him, and giving him his cereal, and, most of all, carrying him around the streets with everybody looking at me and laughing. . . .

Maria said, "You're like Faust's Marguerite." And she began to recite, slowly and rhythmically:

So all alone I was forced to raise her,
This baby girl . . .
At night the little cradle
Stood close to my bed . . .
I gave her water, held her close
To soothe her, or leapt up from the featherbed
When she cried . . .
And then in the morning I would run to the washhouse
And then to the market,
And from the market to the hearth . . .

The basic similarity between the life that was reflected in these verses and my own situation overcame my impatience for a while and made me pay attention. Then Titina, who was greatly amused by this "poetry" that seemed to have been written just for us, asked, "Did you make that up?"

Maria laughed and answered with a self-important air, "Nonsense! Do you think that I know how to write poetry? That's what Marguerite says to Faust; she's talking about her little sister."

"What? That young lady dressed in white, with the long train, worked like that?"

"It was the first women who were so elegantly dressed. Marguerite is just a peasant girl. . . ."

And she began to recite again:

We have no servant; I cook,
sweep, sew, and knit stockings . . .

Titina clapped her hands for joy, laughed loudly, and shrieked, "Goodness, just like us! Just imagine, Denza: that beautiful woman has to work just like us!"

I answered, looking hard at Maria, "Yes, but she had Faust to tell her problems to, and we don't."

Scandalized, Titina reproached me in her usual manner, very harshly, "You're really crazy! What a way to talk!"

Nonetheless, I was determined to make Maria talk at any cost. I said, with a shamelessness that still astounds me when I think of it, "That is, perhaps I do have a Faust, but I don't know him."

I had to endure yet another rebuke from Titina: "You've got a Faust? What stupid thing will you say next? Do us a favor and shut up!"

By now there was no stopping me, and I answered insolently, laughing, "You shut up; you know nothing about it. Maria, have you seen my fat Faust again, the one who was watching me at the opera?"

Maria looked uncertain for a moment, as though she didn't remember, which was extremely embarrassing for me; then she started to laugh and said, "Yes, of course. Didn't I tell you, Giuseppina, that Denza quite dazzled big Mazzucchetti that evening we saw *Faust*?"

That great event—that had so consumed me, changing my mood and my behavior, and my whole view of the future, that had nearly driven me out of my mind—had seemed so inconsequential to Maria that she had not even thought to mention it to her sister!

Giuseppina, however, took the news quite seriously, just as Maria had done that evening, and she said, "My dear, if it's true, listen, that's not a match to sneer at! Since you're so eager to get married in order to get away from home, you should certainly consider him. He's rich, and a nice fellow, too. He always goes to mass with his mother. . . ."

I couldn't help exclaiming bitterly, "There! I told you that if we had gone to mass at Sant' Eufemia, I would have seen him eventually!"

"What? You haven't seen him yet?"

"No. Maria only told me about him after we had left the theater. . . ."

Looking thoughtful, Giuseppina murmured, "How can we point him out to her? What can we do?" Then she broke off her train of thought and observed, "On the other hand, dressed like that, I'm not even sure if it's a good idea to attract his attention. If you could have a dress made that's a little longer . . . and less skimpy than that one, not so tight over the bust . . ."

"Oh, leave my dress out of it; it's not important. Come on, think: how can I get to see that young man?"

Maria, who wasn't inclined to reflection or to wasting time, proposed to introduce him to us at her piano teacher's, who was also his piano teacher, where she would invite us at the same time.

But Giuseppina whispered to her, "You must be dreaming! When has Papa ever allowed us to meet people or go to parties and that sort of thing?"

We went on thinking for a long time; then we finally decided that our cousins would come pick us up the following Sunday to go for a walk on the avenue at the time that the musicians would be playing. When I shook my head in disappointment, anticipating my stepmother's refusing because of the child, Maria settled everything in the following manner:

"And if she says no because of the child, Titina, who never takes care of him, will stay home and babysit. Isn't that right, Titina, for once . . . ? You don't have anyone to see, so you can make this sacrifice for your sister. After all, you'll be better off, too, when she's married. She'll take you out every day; you'll have fun. . . ."

We spent another half hour speculating about what might happen. Then at home followed more days of excitement, of continuous fantasizing on the same theme. Titina, who had been so scandalized at the very idea of a "Faust," ended up taking it seriously, too; we both talked about it as though it were a possible, or even probable, solution to our dilemma.

Hearing us, anyone would have supposed that actual marriage negotiations were going on, and that we were both getting married. For if I were free, my sister would also be free from my stepmother's tyranny, from the tedious child, from everything. She would say to me, bursting with generosity, as though the whole thing were up to her, "You know, it doesn't make any difference to me whether you get married first, even though you're younger. Go ahead: do you think I would want you to lose out on a fortune . . . ?"

I, on the other hand, preferred to talk about him: "I wonder . . . was that the first time he'd seen me that evening at the opera, or had he already seen me before?"

And I said to myself, although I didn't dare tell my sister, that maybe he was in love with me. As for me, I felt that I was in love with him, with this unknown man. I was in love with the lover, with the fact that I had a lover, which made me feel important in my own eyes. It made me feel desirable, and marriageable, like the elegant young ladies who had been to boarding school. I had felt so ashamed of my strange clothes and of our eccentric family ways that this love consoled me and filled me with pride, as though I had been somehow rehabilitated.

Our cousins dropped by in the middle of the week to invite us to go walking on Sunday, as they had promised. And our stepmother didn't even object, as we had foreseen: she said she could take care of the child for a few hours, that we should have a good time, as young people must, that she understood and would always let us, as long as we could do so without any expense to the family.

We accepted her consent and moralizing with feigned indifference, but as soon as our cousins had left we ran to our room in order to give vent to the exclamations of joy and delight that welled up in us.

We hugged each other, laughing and whispering, "How wonderful! We both get to go! How wonderful!"

I added, "So you'll get to see him, too!"

I thought this was quite a privilege for Titina, and that she had me to thank.

After all this hugging and kissing, we felt somewhat awkward, because we weren't used to such demonstrative behavior. We were used to a kiss on either cheek, only upon leaving or returning home when one of us had to leave Novara without the other. This had only happened perhaps two or three times in our memory, when one of us went to visit a married sister of Papa's in Borgomanero.

So mortified were we by the scene that we had made that we didn't dare look at one another. In order to banish the memory, I opened the wardrobe and began to look through my clothes, as though there were really much to choose from.

We rehashed all my sartorial problems, lamenting once again the shabbiness of my wardrobe. And we went on talking about it for the rest of the week, as we undertook small alterations in secret: letting out, ironing, starching, and bluing my dress, all in an attempt to lend it some elegance, along with the addition of a collar and cuffs.

I also had the idea of letting out one of the flounces in the skirt, in order to lengthen it. But on our way out, as we crossed the sunny courtyard, everyone burst out laughing, because my legs showed through the light material of the dress, because I wore only a short petticoat underneath.

So the walk had to be put off for half an hour, while we shortened the flounce again. Not to mention how mortified I felt at looking so foolish in front of our cousins and Signor Bonelli!

Finally we set off, two by two, Maria and I in front, the two elder sisters behind us, and the two fathers bringing up the rear.

Our cousins were all dressed up in cloth capes, with fur muffs and collars; the veils of their hats were pulled down smartly to the tips of their noses, and there emanated from them a wonderful scent of violets, which greatly impressed me.

I walked very awkwardly, with my feet sticking out beneath my skirt and my wrists, red from the cold, showing between my gloves and the ends of my sleeves. For a while I didn't dare say anything, thinking that Maria was probably ashamed to be seen with me, since she said nothing and behaved in a rather haughty way that I had never seen before.

However, the longer I was silent the more humiliated I felt, knowing how silly I must look with my red, sullen face, walking beside that beautiful young woman who could be my mistress. And when we were about to come out on the avenue, I plucked up my courage and asked Maria something I had been wondering about, bending my face closer to hers, so that people could see that we were friends.

"Why did Giuseppina say on Sunday that Mazzucchetti was at the ball with his three friends? Who are they?"

"Oh, DeRossi and Rigamonti. They're always together: people call them the Three Musketeers."

I hadn't the slightest idea who the Three Musketeers were, so without feeling at all embarrassed I revealed how totally mystified I was: "Oh! But who are they?"

Maria said, "Shh!" Then she answered, her hands in her muff, in a very low voice as respectable people do in public (she did not look at me because she would have had to look up, since she was so short), "Don't talk so loudly! The Three Musketeers are characters in a novel. These young men have assumed those three names, and that's what their friends call them."

My natural good sense, reinforced by my stepmother's haranguing for the past two years, rebelled at the very idea. Overcome by incredulity, I forgot to speak softly, "Goodness! Why on earth would they do that?"

This outburst earned me a double reproach, both from Maria and from her sister behind us, who shushed me, too. And then Maria answered, "Speak softly! I don't know why. You know, they read the novel, and they liked those characters. There's also Crosio, who's an officer in the Guides and is home on leave: he's d'Artagnan."

"Who?"

"D'Artagnan. Another Musketeer."

"So they're four of them?"

"Yes. But they're always called 'three' because of the novel."

She said this in the quietest, most controlled tone of voice, barely moving her lips, without the slightest hint of emotion, as though what she was saying were the most natural thing in the world. This girl had the gift of knowing everything and of being surprised at nothing. As for me, I was in such a state of bewilderment that I gave up all hope of understanding. The only thing that interested me in the least was Mazzucchetti. How would we manage to get along? I asked timidly, "And what do they call him? Onorato?"

"Portos, because he's fat . . ."

My eyes opened wide, my mouth gaped open, and I was just about to burst out with "Does 'Portos' mean 'fat'?" when fortunately Maria said, "Shh! Quiet. There he is, but don't look; pretend nothing is happening."

Don't look! When I had come only to see him! I turned my head in every direction, saying, "Where? Where is he?"

"I'm going to tell you, but you must wait before you look; don't let him see you, understand? He's over there, next to the music pavilion, behind the Savi ladies, the ones in the red hats. Don't look yet! He'll greet us, because the piano teacher is there, too, so you'll get to see him."

Behind us Giuseppina whispered softly, "Denza, there they are!"

We always discussed him in the plural. I was as red as a beet with embarrassment, and I was dying to look.

"Are they all there?" I asked.

"Yes. Careful, now they're greeting us."

Out of the corner of my eye I glimpsed movement; I heard the scraping of feet; Maria barely nodded her head, very seriously, without looking at anyone in particular. I looked straight at them, saw hats being doffed, and a group of men in the midst of whom loomed something in a long gray overcoat—a sort of elephant.

My heart fell, and I asked in dismay, "Which one is he?"

"The fattest one. . . . Don't let them see you looking."

I was completely overwhelmed. Such bulk surpassed anything that I could imagine. Of course I knew that they had said he was fat, but I had also tried to play it down, to reconcile his obesity with youth and smartness. . . . Instead, he was a waistless lump, with gigantic, square, high shoulders, a swelling chest, a short neck, and a huge head covered with very smooth black hair, and big, black, bulging eyes. He looked to me like an old man. But as soon as the four of us were seated on a bench away from the music pavilion, while our fathers stood behind us, Maria took from her muff a lovely little handkerchief that smelled of violet and dabbed at her lips, as though to protect them from the cold, and talked to me sensibly, as though we were at home: "Don't talk nonsense! You think he's old? He's twenty-one, and he's really quite handsome. Look—now you can look at him without anyone noticing. See? He has a nice profile. Oh, now he's turning around and looking for you. You must have made a good impression. . . ."

I studied him for a long time. He did, in fact, have a nice profile, reminiscent of a cameo. And when he finally located us, and those big round eyes focused on me for a moment, I found them full of sweetness.

Titina, who was considering him as husband material, was deliberately encouraging. She said, as she leaned around Giuseppina so that I could hear, "You know, he is handsome. He's very distinguished looking."

In fact, whether because that long, light-colored overcoat made him stand out from the others, or because he was a foot taller than they were, he did have a noble air that made him seem their superior. They all addressed him; he answered very calmly, without gesturing. His movements were very slow.

I was able to observe him at leisure, because he had only looked at me for an instant that first time, and then again when they passed by us as I was looking at him, and a third time when he had given me a quick glance as we met under the arches.

On the whole, however, I found him a bit cold, and I felt humiliated and dissatisfied. Maria said that this apparent coldness was proof of his tact, that he did not want to compromise me by looking at me too much. She would find out more from the piano teacher, whether he liked me, what he had said about me.

∞

The next day it began to rain, and it went on raining for ages. As we sat working by the kitchen table, my sister and I talked about him continuously, and about love and marriage; we speculated as to whether we would live with his parents or move into our own house.

I leaned toward the house.

Nonetheless, the thought that he had not looked at me long enough continued to torture me. After what Maria had told me the night of the opera, I had imagined that he had fallen in love like Faust, and by constantly thinking about it I had become convinced that he was obsessed with me body and soul, that he was pining to see me again just as I was pining to see him . . . and that when we did meet his face would express joyful ecstasy, to see his desire finally realized.

Instead, he had remained impassive. In spite of their talk about prudence and not wanting to compromise me, he had struck me as impassive. At our second meeting, I had to admit, his eyes had settled on me with approval, like a caress. And this sustained me.

For the idea that this whole love that I had imagined might have been a dream tormented me; it tormented me to the point where I began to forget his obesity and my first unfavorable impression of him.

The more I reflected, during the monotony of those rainy days in our dreary solitude, the more he touched me.

Once, while I was rocking the child, who was fussy from teething, completely absorbed in my own thoughts—imagining myself already married, alone somewhere with him—I found myself murmuring, to my own surprise, "You poor sweet thing—how fat you are!"

My stepmother, who was cooking, turned and said, "He's certainly not fat anymore, poor thing. Can't you see that this teething is wearing him down?"

She thought I was talking to her child. And, in fact, I had been, in order to give vent to my feelings, but I was talking about *him*. I felt great tenderness at being able to pity him for his obesity, at having something to pardon him, as a proof of my love.

I planted a noisy kiss on the brat's cheek, imagining that I was kissing *him*, and the kid began to scream. I hugged and kissed the brat with unrestrained passion, to the point that my stepmother yelled that I was choking him and took him away from me.

I ran into my room, threw myself on my bed, and cried my heart out with my face in the pillow. It was that day that the process of falling in love was complete. From that day on his fatness, his short neck, his shiny, straight hair all seemed beautiful to me, and I would feel an overwhelming tenderness course through me when he appeared in my thoughts, as he did constantly.

One evening, when the child was already in bed, my father and stepmother were drinking chamomile tea next to the fire in their room (as they did every evening at bedtime), and we were behind the screen saying goodnight to our aunt, the doorbell rang. We heard our father's footsteps going to answer the doorbell, then the sound of happy, pleasant, soft voices:

"Oh, goodness, sir . . . a man like you going to bed at this hour! For shame!"

It was Maria's voice: our cousins were here. The tedium of the unceasing rain had driven them out to see us. I became very excited and turned quite red. Of course, the piano teacher had answered them, and they had come to tell me.

I ran into Papa's room with shining eyes, winking at my cousins as I greeted them, as though to say, with a knowing air, *I understand; I know why you've come; we'll talk soon.*

And they smiled and winked graciously at me, and shook my hand so energetically that my arm shook all the way to my shoulder.

I waited until the old people's conversation was well under way, then I said, as a pretext for getting away, "Have you seen that skirt border that we're embroidering?"

"Of course! We've seen it several times. Don't you remember?"

Giuseppina said this in astonishment, as though she did not understand why I had made such a proposal.

I waited for a while, then, because it wasn't possible to whisper, I tried again. "Do you want to see the baby sleeping?"

All three girls repeated, like a triple echo, ". . . the baby sleeping!!!" They looked at me, stupefied. It was so unusual for us to show the slightest admiration for the brat, whom we always called "the little old man," that they did not know what to think. But I insisted, "Maria, you love children. . . ." I stood up and strode resolutely to the cradle. My cousins and Titina followed me. There I began to rhapsodize over how cute he was, how he had dimples on his arms, so that my stepmother would overhear, then I said softly to Maria, "So? What did he say?"

"Who?"

This time I lost my patience and I mumbled angrily, "Lord,

you never remember anything! What do you think? What did Faust say to the piano teacher?"

"Oh, that's right! I haven't asked him yet."

I got so angry that I could have hit her. In fact, I think that I really did hit her, because I stumbled here and there in order to get away from them and went back and sat by the fire without saying anything more. They followed me and sat down in bewilderment. Later, as they were leaving, Maria whispered to me as she pressed my hand, "Come on. I'll ask him at my next lesson. I didn't know if you really liked him."

But I had lost faith in her promises; I was disillusioned; I felt that I had no one to support me in attaining what I longed for. I saw my love slipping away, and I desired it with all the ardor with which one longs for a fleeting dream.

However, I did not find these sufferings unbearable, like those that I hated so much that involved my stepmother, the house, and the child. This kind of suffering was dear to me; I enjoyed it. When Titina, seeing me thoughtful and sad, often on the verge of tears, would say, "Pray to the Madonna that she will let you forget him," I would get angry and distressed at the idea of forgetting such a love: that it should no longer be in my mind or heart, that I should lose that sweetness that filled the whole of me, and be left with that great emptiness, that great silence. And I would cry, "No, no, please, don't, I beg you! When I've forgotten him, then what?"

∞

One Saturday night the child got very sick with the usual teething problems. We all had to get up to prepare herbal remedies and plasters, and we were up all night.

In the morning he was still sick; he was running a fever and he wanted his mother to hold him. Our aunt had not been out all winter, because she had rheumatism in one leg and couldn't walk. Papa had to run to the doctor's, to the pharmacist's, and to church in order to light a candle to the Madonna so that the child would get better. The result was that there was no one to accompany us to mass and, as much as our stepmother and Papa objected to "the practice of leaving the girls in the care of a servant who was more or less their own age, and less educated," for once they had to give in and send us to mass with the servant.

My plan was already formed when they had barely uttered these words. In fact, I must confess that even during the previous night, in the middle of the child's crying and the general hand-wringing, I was hounded by the single idea that so dominated me and I kept repeating to myself: "Tomorrow they certainly won't be able to go to mass with us. If they let us go with the servant . . ." And though I wasn't happy that the poor "little old man" was sick, I did find it consoling that since it had to happen it had happened on a Saturday night.

I said nothing at home in order to avoid any argument, but as soon as we were out on the street I said to Titina: "Let's go to mass at Sant' Eufemia!"

She didn't argue. We agreed to instruct the servant not to tell anyone, and we set off in a hurry, because the church was quite far away.

When we went in, the mass had already begun. The priest was already reading the epistle. As we opened the door, we bumped into the colossal figure of my Faust, who was standing right next to the door, as young men often do, perhaps to show that they are there against their will and that they're impatient to leave.

He watched us enter, following us with his eyes as we looked for seats, and, when I had found one not far away so that I could see him, he turned toward us, ignoring the altar. I did the same. I watched him intensely, crazily, throughout the mass.

With my arduous eyes fixed on his, I told him of my long love, of my suffering and pain, of the joy of that moment, of my sweet hopes for the future, and of my faith in him. I felt that I was telling him all of this, and that he understood.

It was a wonderful day, and I drew from it a well of comfort and joy that got me through the rest of the child's illness and the rainy season. I would discuss the most banal domestic trifles in a joyful, animated voice; I would smile blissfully at the whining baby, and the pile of diapers waiting to be washed, and the kitchen pots, and I held my head gloriously high.

Finally I was sure of being loved, and he knew that his feelings were reciprocated. We had entered into an agreement. It was now but a question of time.

∽

After that morning at mass, every time that I encountered Mazzucchetti in the street—besides blushing and feeling my heart beating like a hammer—I gave him a secret smile, looking him in the eye with a knowing air. I had a right to do so. And he would look at me insistently; if he was in front he would turn and look back from time to time. I would count the number of times he turned around. If it was evening and only my father was with us, I would turn and look at him as we passed each other and went off in opposite directions. And sometimes he would have stopped in his tracks, turning back to look at me. One day when this happened I was carrying the child and my stepmother was behind us; I stopped to tell her that the child's hands were hot and that perhaps he was sick— just to be able to turn around for a moment to look at my lover.

The child was cool and just fine, so I caught a long lecture on my fecklessness, of which not one word penetrated.

Such were the stages of my love, in which my sister and my cousins and I found ample matter for conversation and I for tireless meditation, both day and night. They sufficed to nourish my hopes, or rather to strengthen my faith.

Gradually other more important events took place, which occupied us at great length. The first thing was that Maria found occasion to ask the piano teacher casually if he had seen me that day that we had all walked on the avenue. He had, adding that I was "a fine, strapping young woman." So Maria had whispered, "Mazzucchetti was with you, wasn't he, Maestro?"

"Yes, he and DeRossi, and Rigamonti, and Crosio: the usual band of Musketeers."

"And what did they say about my cousin?"

"I don't know what the others said; I was in back with big Mazzucchetti, Portos . . ."

"Didn't he say anything? I thought that he was looking at her. . . ."

"Yes, he said that she was beautiful. She's just the sort of woman that he likes."

"Oh, really? Why?"

"Because he's a bit awkward socially; he doesn't like formality, and elegant women intimidate him."

From this we concluded that I must also suit him perfectly as a prospective bride: for, if he had only wanted to look at me, it wouldn't have mattered to him in the slightest whether I was elegant or not.

The other events were the following:

One day, when I was on the Bonellis' balcony, Mazzucchetti turned around three times to look up as he crossed the street, and he stopped for several minutes before he turned the corner. Titina even claimed that he had nodded his head in greeting, but our cousins didn't think so because, as they said, "men greet women by taking off their hats, not by nodding."

Late one evening at the end of the summer, as I was going out with Papa, we saw him standing alone in front of our door. This event was crucial, and it kept me happily absorbed during the entire month that I spent in Borgomanero visiting my father's sister (my stepmother thought that I was losing my rustic bloom and that therefore I needed more oxygen in the air I breathed).

In Borgomanero, having neither Titina nor my cousins to discuss my love with, I ended up confiding in my aunt's daughter, since she was engaged to the son of the local pharmacist, an apprentice in a pharmacy in Novara, who wrote her every week. My cousin, who didn't hesitate to inform the entire town of her own love life, immediately told her mother about mine, and that evening at supper my aunt told her husband: "You know, Remigio, our Denza has told us some good news: she's engaged to a very rich young man, from a good family in Novara."

I grew hot and sweaty. This had gone further than I thought it would. I was terrified that they would congratulate Papa when he came to get me, and—although at the moment I accepted their good wishes and felt a new thrill in my role as a bride—then I spent a sleepless night worrying over what would happen if they were to mention this to my family.

The next morning I begged my cousin to tell her mother not to say anything yet to my father, because neither he nor my stepmother knew about it.

"What?" she exclaimed. "You're engaged, and your family doesn't know it?"

I had to get myself out of this somehow, and I had come up with an answer during the night.

"I'm not really engaged, you understand; I didn't say that. It's almost certain that we'll get married, because we're in love, but it's my cousins the Bonellis who have arranged everything."

"Are they friends of his?"

"They take lessons from the same piano teacher."

"And he told your cousins that he wants to marry you?"

"He said as much to the piano teacher, who told us . . ."

I knew I was telling a pack of lies, but they were little white ones, and I was able to assuage my conscience. Besides, my purpose was not to save the world, but only myself and my love, which was far more important to me than the world. And I intended to go to confession.

Nonetheless, the formal declaration that bound my cousin to her fiancé, and their regular letters, all ending with "with undying love from your Antonio," had given me new aspirations.

I returned to Novara filled with an intense desire for a letter, or a promise. Titina said that it would have been better if Mazzucchetti had simply asked for my hand and married me, but I wanted some letters first. I would compose one in my head and read it over. It was not quietly affectionate, like Antonio's to my cousin: instead, it was ardent, as first declarations of love should be. Sometimes, I would think in such passionate language that my eyes filled with tears.

⌒

Finally we met and talked: here is what happened on that memorable day. It was the first Sunday in October, the Feast of the Rosary. After vespers there was a procession in San Martino, a neighboring village, in which the Madonna of the Rosary was carried about, dressed in gold with a crown of pearls.

The Bonellis had a house in the center of San Martino, but you couldn't see the procession from it. However, at the far end of town they owned a farmhouse, with a long balcony overlooking the street; on that autumn afternoon they invited us over to view the procession, which was to pass right in front of the house.

This gave us an opportunity to talk freely about my beloved, because in this village there was no probability of meeting Mazzucchetti or anyone else. The local young men never went beyond the city gates. That day Papa had to go with my step-mother to visit an old relative of hers, from whom she apparently had hopes of inheriting money, so he let us go with our cousins and Signor Bonelli.

The four of us girls were on the balcony, watching the crowd of peasants dressed in their holiday best, and the cross at the head of the procession advancing from the far end of the main street, when from the opposite direction—almost as though they had emerged from the countryside—there suddenly appeared the group of Mazzucchetti, his three friends, and the piano teacher. We were at the far end of town, and they soon disappeared under the balcony and were about to pass by without seeing us. But Maria shouted, "Maestro! Maestro!" And when the teacher raised his head and looked up, she called, "Do come up!"

What an event! I had not yet recovered from the shock of seeing him in that unexpected place, of fearing that he would pass by without seeing me, and there he was, standing beneath the balcony with his large eyes fixed on me, next to someone who was talking to my cousin. It was almost as though *we* were talking; in fact, he and his friends removed their hats and we bowed our heads in greeting.

And that wasn't all. Our cousins, who were so proper in the city, were quite beside themselves at running into respectable people in the country. Maria kept saying to the piano teacher: "Come on up! Don't you see? The procession is almost here."

The teacher indicated his friends, and said with a shrug, "I'm not alone."

So that amazing girl called down: "Come up, all of you!" Then turning to his friends, whom she had only seen at balls and knew only slightly: "Do come in! *A la guerre comme à la guerre!*"

She even knew French! Once again the four hats swept grandly off the four heads; then they all disappeared into the doorway beneath. A minute later the wooden balcony shook beneath the footsteps of Mazzucchetti who, like the well-bred young man he was, passed me without stopping and went to greet the young ladies of the house.

Giuseppina, who had better manners than her sister, didn't lose her head just because she was in the country; after a round of vigorous handshaking she said, "Where's Papa? Maestro, do go in and get our father."

In the meantime Maria had turned toward us; she said, indicating the gentlemen, "Signor DeRossi, Signor Rigamonti, Signor Crosio, Signor Mazzucchetti." Then with a graceful little gesture she indicated Titina and me and went on, "The Signorine Dellara."

Not only had I never seen anyone make an introduction before, I didn't even know that it was done. Maria was destined to astonish me over and over again. What's more, I thought that this was a completely original idea of hers—this getting us to know each other, so that we could smooth over any awkwardness and talk to each other. And I thought it was a wonderful invention, and I admired in my little cousin the brilliance of that unknown, remote inventor.

The gentlemen all bowed; presently Signor Bonelli came in; everyone shook hands and talked loudly; then Maria implored us to be quiet, because the procession was coming. Actually, it was already there beneath us, so we all looked down, and Mazzucchetti was standing right next to me. My heart was beating so hard that it felt as though it would jump out of my chest, and I felt proud and happy, as though I were formally engaged. After a while, when the loud notes of the *tantum ergo,* sung off-key by the peasants in the procession, drowned out our voices, he asked me rather mysteriously, "Are you having a good time?" and he looked me in the eye as though to say, *Tell me the truth. It's a matter of life and death.*

I said yes, and it rang out so loudly and joyfully that it was as though he had asked me: *Will you take this man to be your lawful wedded husband?*

There followed a long, awkward pause, during which I felt that he was preparing to say something.

Then even more mysteriously than before, he whispered, "I saw you one morning at mass at Sant' Eufemia, I believe, this spring. . . ."

I corrected him: "It was barely March."

"How well you remember!"

"Yes. I do have a good memory."

I gave him a quick glance as I said this, meaning *in circumstances like these*. And he understood, because he looked at me intently, the look of a man in love, and continued, "But you've never come to Sant' Eufemia again."

"No. It's too far. . . . My stepmother won't let me."

What he meant—what his eyes and voice said—was: *Would you like to see me again, and look at each other the way we did then?*

And I answered that unspoken question frankly, as seriously and as deeply moved as if I had actually confessed my love to him, "Yes, I would."

"Thank you," he whispered, and with that we had said everything. We had understood each other, and we were both moved. The baldachin was passing with the sacrament. The peasants were all kneeling in the street. Titina fell to her knees. I was about to do the same thing, but I glanced at my cousins and, seeing that they had bowed their heads low but had remained standing, and that the men on the balcony were standing, I did likewise. In the midst of the wave of scent and smoke that arose from the censers that were being shaken around the baldachin, I heard Mazzucchetti whisper lovingly, almost in my ear, "Denza, will you allow me to write to you?"

Denza! He had called me by my first name! This gave me such a pang of love and joy that it seemed like pain and made me cry. The letter that I had dreamed of! But how could I receive it? That was impossible until we were formally engaged, with my father's approval. I answered sorrowfully, "I can't receive letters. My father and stepmother would have to read them first."

I said this to imply that he would be able to write me after he had talked to them. He didn't insist; instead he asked when he could see me, where I went to mass. Without hesitating, I told him that I went to the Duomo, and that our pew was to the right of the main nave, in front of the chapel of Sant' Agapito. . . . And he said, "On Sunday I'll come to the Duomo."

Then there was a long silence. I felt, however, that he still had something else to say, because I, too, felt that something was missing, even though we had said it in so many words. But the procession was over: Signor Bonelli had brought in bottles of white wine from the house in town; all of the guests had gathered inside around the door to the balcony, while the two of us remained outside. A peasant came up behind us, carrying a tray full of glasses, tapped Mazzucchetti on the shoulder, and brought us abruptly back down to earth from our paradise of love.

We each took a glass and stood there holding it awkwardly, not daring to indulge in such a physical act as drinking, and yet wanting to break the spell. He was braver: he stood in a daze for a minute, then downed his wine in one gulp and went inside to put down his glass.

Once alone, I felt rather mortified to have gone off and staged this love scene in front of everyone, and I went inside to my cousins who were chatting with the young men while Titina listened, openmouthed, in the background.

DeRossi and Maria were having a disjointed, incomprehensible conversation. She was saying, "Even ice melts when the sun gets very hot."

And he answered, "But not glaciers . . ."

Maria said very slyly, "Glaciers are deceptive, you know. Etna has fire inside. . . ."

And Giuseppina chimed in, with that rather disparaging elegant-beauty air of hers, "And tonight I think that Etna is erupting."

They all burst out laughing and moved away. I couldn't understand what was so funny, or how they could be so interested in a mountain that no one had seen.

Maria turned around and saw me; taking my arm, she said, "Did you hear that? They think he's a glacier."

"Goodness! But what do you care? I thought she was talking about Etna."

She answered, "It doesn't matter, to me. I was thinking of *you*. In my opinion, he's been quite the opposite of a glacier this evening. Did he propose?"

As usual, my friend never ceased to amaze me. "What? You mean you were talking about *him?* Is he the glacier with fire inside? What a way of talking you have!"

"No, it's DeRossi who thinks he's cold as ice, incapable of falling in love . . . but it doesn't matter. What did he say?"

As I repeated the conversation I realized that he had actually said very little, but that he had implied a great deal. And Maria agreed with me. That "Thank you" and "On Sunday I'll come to the Duomo" were both a declaration of love and a promise. What on earth could that man be thinking, calling him a glacier?

We all went out together, walking toward the city. Crosio, the handsome officer on leave, walked beside Giuseppina; they spoke little, in low voices, and looked like a king and queen.

Maria took Titina's arm, and the two other young men fluttered around them, and we heard the murmur of conversation and happy laughter.

Our uncle, who devotedly accompanied his daughters everywhere, who adored them and thought of nothing but pleasing them, and who spoke little and then only of business or politics, brought up the rear with the piano teacher. As we passed them, I heard my uncle discussing the Cavour Canal.

I was in front of everybody, and Mazzucchetti was beside me. The main road was quite wide. The others in the group kept to the right; we stayed to the left.

Under the cover of falling darkness, he found the courage to pronounce those missing words: "You do know that I love you very much?"

"Yes."

Then I felt something moving down the folds of my dress, and he took my hand, which was hanging by my side, and squeezed it. In that moment, a shudder of tenderness went through me; in my heart I felt a pang of utter joy, which must be the greatest of all human pleasures. I have never known anything that surpassed or even equaled it. And, like Faust, I would have sold my soul for him to have dared to embrace me. We were both so moved that we fell into a long silence. He was the first to break it, saying that he was very sorry that we couldn't write to each other, because he would have told me all his secrets. By way of an answer, I asked, "Do you have secrets?"

He said that he did and, urging me to the greatest secrecy, he confided that he and his three friends were the Musketeers. For a number of years they had rented a room, which happened to be near our house. They went there in the evenings, put on fezzes and smoked their pipes, and they called themselves Athos, Portos, Aramis, and d'Artagnan. He was Portos.

In fact, he remembered seeing me one evening as I was leaving the house with my father and sister, just as he was waiting, as usual, to meet his friends. . . . That was the evening that we had fantasized over, because he had been standing at our door! This was a moment of bitterness, in the midst of such great joy: he had not been there because of me.

He spoke to me in a low voice tinged with a kind of sad gravity, like a man who is involved in a conspiracy, who accepts the fatality that hangs over him and knows its dangers. I had heard that story and knew that it was generally known. As he told it, however, it took on a completely different significance. The others hadn't told me about the rented room, the pipes, or the fezzes: they didn't know about that. Nobody did: I was the only one who was being told. He was making me privy to a secret. I planned to guard it jealously in my heart, and I was proud of this proof of his trust.

I would only have liked for my cousins to know of his confidences, and also that idiot who called him a glacier. . . .

Then he confided that he was a man marked by fate, and he offered proof: one day, when he had been out hunting with his friends, they had met an old woman whom he described as bent over, toothless, and hoarse, like the old women in novels. They had asked her to tell their fortunes in return for a lira from each.

He, of course, was a strong person, who scorned all superstition; he was even something of an atheist . . . yes, he was, a bit. He hid it so as not to upset his mother, but in his heart he made fun of gullible people. And yet, he had recognized in the old woman's words the solemn ring of truth, and it had disturbed him deeply—he, Portos, the strong one! What's more, a storm had sprung up, and it was thundering and lightning!

The old lady had predicted that he would be the ruin of the woman whom he fell in love with, and who fell in love with him. Therefore, he swore to me that of his own accord he would never have made the slightest attempt to approach me, no matter how much he wanted to; if fate had not caused us to meet that evening, perhaps we would never have even spoken!

I felt a shiver go through my entire body at this idea. He went on talking about his fatalism! Since chance had brought us together in this "nearly miraculous" way, it was proof that he had to declare his feelings, and he had done so, whatever the risk might be.

But he was sad and fearful for me—only on my account—in the midst of his joy, and only fate could be blamed for his dilemma; he was not personally responsible, because in fact he felt that the old woman had spoken the truth. He did bring bad luck, especially to people whom he loved. He used to have a sister, but she died at sixteen!

He added, "I would have liked to write you all this."

After a pause, during which he seemed to be mulling over the fine words he might have written, which were now lying idle in his brain, he asked, "Do you forgive me, Denza?"

I pressed the hand that was still holding mine, managing to communicate a sort of feverish ardor, then I asked, "And what's your first name?"

"Onorato. Call me Onorato when you speak of me, or think of me. . . ."

Meanwhile, we had reached the city gates. He stopped, saying, "Good-bye, Denza." And his hand seemed like a sentient being with a heart and mind, so much did it say and so many feelings did it convey in that last trembling, nervous squeeze. That hand, too, told me that I should call him by his first name. So I whispered, a bit embarrassed, "Good-bye, Onorato."

All the others had caught up with us and stopped of one accord. We had to separate. If we had all entered Novara together, who knew what the gossips would have said, and how long it would have gone on!

We all felt this, although nobody said anything, and we shook hands all around as we parted, but without exchanging any invitations or promises to visit. And between the two of us there was nothing more to say.

The old woman's prediction did leave me somewhat apprehensive. Not that I believed it in the slightest: no one could ever have convinced me that anything as wonderful as being loved, and having someone tell you that he loves you, could bring you bad luck. What frightened me, though, was the thought that *he* believed it and that, perhaps, owing to his groundless fear, he might not try to approach me or have anything to do with me, and would deprive me of so much joy. . . . I would have liked to convince him that until now he had been the source of nothing but infinite sweetness, that his every look and smile filled me with happiness, and that it was impossible for such bliss to bring me bad luck, and that to me the only bad luck was to be separated from him. . . .

Titina asked, like the optimistic girl that she was, "When will he ask Papa for your hand?"

I don't know why that question struck me as offensive to Onorato, as though it implied distrust, and I answered with great dignity, "When he wants to. Do you think that I don't trust him, that I need him to talk to my family and bind himself to me with a promise, in order to believe that he loves me? I know that he loves me, that 'he is mine and I am his': that's enough to make me happy."

My sister, who had firm opinions, persisted with: "If I were you, I'd rather have him marry me."

"Not me. You don't know how wonderful it is to have someone who loves you, whom you get along with, whose secrets you know. . . . Before, I couldn't wait to get married, either. But now that I've experienced such happiness, I want to savor it, make it last a bit longer, before I marry him."

In fact, for the moment—having gotten over the doubts that had tormented me and the anxiety about meeting him, blissful in the sense of security and trust that his love gave me—I was too absorbed in my new happiness to even notice the irritations of my life at home, which had made me want to get married in the past. I was happy in the midst of all these annoyances, precisely as though they did not exist.

My most ardent desire at this time was to read *The Three Musketeers,* in order to understand better the secret that he carried deep inside him. But this was a pleasure that I wasn't destined to have. Maria wanted to lend me the novel, but Giuseppina was firmly opposed. She knew that my father was very strict about what he allowed us to read, and she absolutely did not want either her sister or herself to be responsible for my reading a novel without his knowledge. She said, "Ask your father if he would allow it."

I couldn't even imagine asking him such a thing, much less his allowing it!

∽

Autumn arrived. A rainy, dreary autumn, which we spent cooped up in the house, with our stern stepmother, our father who was completely wrapped up in her, the whiny little boy, and our rheumatic aunt.

However, when the house was filled with the noise of housework and the child's shrieks, and during the afternoon when it was as silent and sad as a tomb, I would hear Onorato's breathless, loving voice ringing in my ears, repeating over and over that sweet, precious refrain: "You do know that I love you very much? And you, you do love me just a little, don't you? Good-bye, Denza!"

Sometimes I was moved to tears; sometimes I would laugh and sing and play crazy games with my little brother, in order to give vent to the joyful feelings that welled up in me, but I was always happy.

One evening I happened to enter my stepmother's room unannounced. As I was about to open the door I heard her saying to my father, "How strange! I thought that Denza would have more suitors. Now that she's lost her rustic bloom, and has more of a poetic quality, she really is a lovely young woman. And yet no one is courting her, or proposing. . . ."

My father answered, "That's hardly surprising, is it? Girls without dowries are seldom much in demand." After a while he added, "A while ago Bonelli mentioned something about Mazzucchetti, the engineer's son. It seems that he looks at her very favorably. . . ."

"Nonsense! Everyone probably looks at her favorably: she's a beautiful girl, a pleasure to look at. But don't think for a minute that Mazzucchetti means to marry her. A man who must have a million lire! He'll look at her as long as he has nothing better to do, then he'll marry someone else. . . ."

I retreated instead of going in, laughing inwardly at my stepmother's blunder, which was contrary to her usual good sense. If only they knew, I thought! If only they knew that everything is already settled between us, and that it's only a matter of time! That I know his secrets, and call him Onorato!

And in my heart I felt that unshakable faith that the Bible says can move mountains.

Autumn passed, and winter came, a harsh winter with snowfalls that blocked the streets, and our house, where only the kitchen fireplace and the one in our stepmother's room were lit, was as cold as Siberia. I got chilblains on my hands, which got shamefully red and swollen.

I reflected, however, that these were the hands that Onorato had pressed so lovingly, and I contemplated them in ecstasy; even deformed as they were, they evoked in me enchanting visions of that unforgettable evening.

Carnival came around, too, our gossipy, pretentious little provincial Carnival, during which everyone discussed the most insignificant parties, both before and after, making the most minute inventories of what other people were wearing, and everyone overdressed.

The Bonellis, who were very much sought after, always talked about their parties and outings; I didn't have the slightest idea what they were talking about. And yet, I had no desire for such amusements. What would I have done at a dance? Aside from the fact that I didn't know how to dance, the idea of dancing with other men besides him horrified me as much as being unfaithful. And he didn't dance. People said it was because he was too fat, but I was sure that he didn't dance because I wasn't present. And I also attributed to him, aside from momentary disappointment at not being able to embrace me as we waltzed, great admiration for the reclusive life that I was leading, and for my modesty.

I remembered what Maria's piano teacher had said that time: that he was something of a social misfit, that elegant young women intimidated him. "He's intimidated" was the piano teacher's polite way of saying that his pupils were so very elegant. But a rich, handsome man like Onorato shouldn't be intimidated by anyone. Which just meant that he didn't like them—he liked simple, modest girls, and there wasn't anyone who was simpler or more modest than I was.

Knowing his preference, I forgot all my old complaints about my family's patriarchal customs, and I began to feel that I was the one who had deliberately chosen this way of life and who preferred it.

∽

Instead of Carnival, we celebrated the eight days of San Gaudenzio. Beginning on January 22, which was the feast of San Gaudenzio, the first bishop of Novara, a benediction service with musical accompaniment was celebrated daily for a week, and professors even came from the Orchestra of La Scala in Milan.

We had a front-row pew, to the left of the high altar. In front of us was a large, empty space, where men stood to see the musicians by the organ, to the right of the altar. Every year we went regularly to the week-long celebration, no matter what the weather was like. We cared nothing for the ritual, little for the mass, and least of all for the saint. But at least we saw a few people, and some young men looked at us, which was something in the monotony of our existence.

Usually our aunt accompanied us, because our stepmother didn't care for music, and our father always spent his evenings with her. Besides, church was our aunt's domain. That year I started to worry a month ahead of time that her rheumatism would prevent her from going out. But that week represented the most festive time of the year for her, too, and she took such good care of herself that by the time the feast day arrived she was in relatively good health.

On the very first evening, a few minutes after I had come in, hearing the click of footsteps I raised my eyes, my heart beating wildly: the Musketeers were entering slowly, Portos in the lead, the others following. He walked over and leaned against the wall beneath the pulpit right in front of me, and the others lined up beside him.

He looked me straight in the eyes and went on watching me intently, tirelessly, all through the service. His friends all looked at me, too, as though they were all in love with me. Even when I happened to run into them on the street when they were not together, they would look at me and then turn around to look at me some more, just as he did. And I felt as though I had become a fifth member of their fraternity, and I loved all of them as brothers, because of him.

The next evening, and on every one thereafter, he returned at the same time, with the same friends; he would stand in the same place, and give me the same long, intense looks. On the second evening, however, something else happened. At the moment of the benediction—as the priest raised the ciborium containing the sacrament and the censers were emitting clouds of smoke and incense and everybody bowed their heads in reverence—I slowly raised mine and looked at Onorato.

He had had the same idea and was looking at me. In that deep, solemn silence, our eyes—as though isolated and alone, over those bent heads, in that heady scent of incense, that mysterious light, that place of prayer—met in one ardent look of love: a long merging of souls, an embrace, a kiss.

When the priest's off-key voice, followed immediately by the high, festive voices of the musicians, intoned the *O salutaris hostia*, I roused as though from a long embrace—dazed, confused, and drunk. I felt even more inexorably bound to him, as though I belonged to him.

Throughout the entire eight days, we would raise our heads at the moment of the benediction and repeat that sort of mute, ardent duet of love, which left me in a sort of guilty agitation, but wildly happy. Throughout my life, the lofty silence of the benediction has reminded me of the joy of that time, moving me to tears. My family and friends have an exaggerated notion of my religious convictions.

When that week was over I felt a great loss, as though some terrible catastrophe like a fire or flood had taken place, which had deprived me of countless treasures and plunged me into the depths of gloom.

Nevertheless, I saw Onorato without fail at Sunday mass, and I often met him in the street. If we went to tea at the Bonellis, my cousins would take me out on the balcony where I sometimes saw him pass by, and he always looked at me in the same way.

Then during Lent, my sister and I took turns going to church with my aunt. And he was always there, at the head of the row of pews where we sat in the chapel of Sant' Agapito. When it was my turn to go to church he would look at me all during the sermon, and when it was Titina's turn he would look at her and she would tell me about him when she came back, bearing those looks as though she were bringing me back a message, which was also a delight.

Moreover, my case was not an isolated one. There were quite a few young women with love stories like mine in Novara, who were just as happy and trustful as I was, and who went on that way for years, without asking anything more of their lovers or receiving anything from them.

A pharmacist's daughter across the street from us had waited for a notary's son for thirteen years before she had married him. True, she had died of some nervous disease little more than a year later, but this couldn't happen to me. These love affairs "of the eyes" are so much a part of life in Novara that, when speaking of middle-class lovers, we often say, "Mr. X is looking at Miss Y." Only when referring to working-class people and shopkeepers do we say, "So-and-so is talking to so-and-so."

All over the Novara region there is a custom of giving people a little saw halfway through Lent. Members of the lower classes draw a saw on someone's back or wrap the saw up and hide it on a person in some ingenious way, so that the object of the joke isn't aware of it. They find this very amusing. Gentlemen send ladies elegant saws, which are a pretext for giving some trinket, or a painting, or some other little gift.

Gallant gentlemen use the saws to court young ladies whom they have met at the balls during Carnival. They send them in letters through the mail, accompanied by declarations of love in poetry and prose, which remain anonymous only to the young ladies' families. The recipients immediately guess the writers' identities.

On that day at the midpoint of Lent the Bonellis received bundles of letters, with saws cut out of paper, or painted, or made of embroidered silk, or silver. . . . They had each even received lovely little gold saws, which they always wore dangling from their watch chains.

That year, on the twentieth day of Lent, when the servant came back from marketing she brought up a letter that she had gotten from the doorkeeper. It was addressed to me: "Denza Dellara!" I felt the blood rush to my cheeks in a blaze of heat. Titina grew pale. She told me afterward that she had thought this was his formal proposal of marriage. Imagine, since it was addressed to me! But that was her obsession.

My sister, stepmother, and I were all standing around the kitchen table. The letter was on the table, between an open package of meat and a wet cabbage, which was dripping on it. I devoured the letter with my eyes, not daring to touch it.

When my stepmother had gotten the bills from the servant, she picked up the envelope in a leisurely fashion and said, as she went to her room to get her glasses, "It's probably something silly. This is Saw Day!" I was well aware of what day it was: I had been thinking about this day for months, praying for this letter, without daring to voice my hopes even to my sister, since they might well have been in vain.

My stepmother came back with her glasses on her nose and the open letter in her hand; she read it next to the window, then said with a shrug, "I said it was probably just something silly." And with that she threw it back on the table, along with a saw in very pale turquoise, which stuck to the wet piece of beef. The letter had seemed so innocuous to her that she was giving it back to me.

Forcing a smile, I asked, nervous and trembling, "May I read it?"

"Go ahead! You can be proud to receive such fashionable letters."

I picked up the sheet of paper that was dripping with cabbage water and read:

> Un dì felice.
> One happy, celestial day
> You appeared before me,
> And from that first moment
> I have burned with immense love.

With that love that throbs with the entire universe
Mysterious and lofty,
The heart's cross and delight.

My stepmother was looking at me, expecting me to laugh, too, and say how silly it was. But I was so upset that I couldn't breathe; I tried to laugh, but instead I burst into a flood of tears.

Probably suspecting something, my stepmother asked, more gently than usual, "What's the matter? Do you know who wrote it?"

Choking with sobs, I shook my head and shoulders violently.

She went on, "No? Too bad! I wish you did, because if he were a nice young man with honorable intentions, a good match, we could see what he has to say and try to arrange a marriage. It's time to break the ice."

My hopes fell. The idea that Onorato might be approached by someone who would force him to marry me, as though he were paying a tax, made me blush and filled me with fear. I felt that he would think that I was part of a conspiracy to force his consent, and that he would be offended and avoid me. I wanted him to approach me of his own accord, when his circumstances permitted, and I wanted to give him some significant, unequivocal proof of my faith in him, by not ever asking him about his intentions. How could I doubt them?

My stepmother continued, "If you don't know who wrote this foolishness then I don't understand why you're crying. . . ."

Titina answered, astonishing me with her ready wit, "She knows it's a joke, and she's ashamed."

I nodded in agreement, and took advantage of this explanation to reread the letter, and cry my eyes out in a fit of nervous emotion.

My stepmother gave me an affectionate cuff and said, "And you're crying because of a joke? A big plump wench like you? Let them talk! When I was your age, I was at a party, wearing a lovely new pink dress for the first time, with a white tulle collar and a little silk jacket. . . . I met a group of young men who looked at me, and then the leader said, 'Everything's nice except her face.' But that didn't make me cry. I laughed, too, and it cheered me up. Furthermore, maybe it's someone who's really in love with you! And sooner or later, he may come along and propose. He has a rather silly way of going about things, but so what? You don't have to be a genius to get married. Come on, stop crying and go wash your face."

It seemed like a miracle to be able to run to my room and reread those old words, which I had known and sung to myself for so long, and then kiss them and reread them once again.

∞

During the spring and for part of the summer nothing else happened.

Toward the middle of June, on one terribly hot evening, as we passed the Café Cavour, I saw Onorato with his three friends, sitting at a table in the midst of an elegant crowd. Waiters were running around with trays held high, shouting, "Right away! Coming!"

We had never been to that elegant café. The few times that we went out for ice cream we went to a modest, less frequented café, and we went in through the back door into an empty room. And we ordered three bowls of ice cream and two extra dishes; then we divided them. My father and stepmother would each give part of their ice cream to the little boy in a dish. Titina would divide hers with me. Moreover, the waiter would bring only three spoons, and Papa would have to insist and get mad in order to get two more. I think the waiter was making fun of us.

That evening, perhaps because she was delirious with the heat, my stepmother suggested that we stop at the Café Cavour. I blushed at the thought of making such a fuss over dishes in front of all those people and *him*, but I couldn't refuse. So I said that I had a headache and couldn't have ice cream, so only Titina had to share hers with the boy, and there were no further complications.

I felt that there was something unusual about Onorato's gaze that evening, that his expression was one of bitterness or melancholy. Twice he bowed his head slightly in greeting. When we got up, so did he, and naturally the other Musketeers followed suit; we could hear them talking behind us all the way home. And while Papa was opening the front door, they passed by; after a few steps Mazzucchetti turned around and bowed to me; *he definitely did bow.*

The effect that this encounter had on me was not entirely positive. I was upset. I felt that he meant to tell me something, something sad. But what? Titina wouldn't help me guess; she would say, "You're crazy! It's always the same story: he looked at you just the way he always does. It would be better if you got married!"

I didn't see him for a few days. On Sunday he didn't come to mass, for the first time in nearly a year! And that same evening I met two of the Musketeers by themselves. DeRossi and Rigamonti . . . Portos and d'Artagnan were missing.

This was too much! I began to mope, to imagine terrible things, although Titina insisted that he must have gone to take "the waters that make you lose weight, but that make him get fatter." I couldn't stop worrying.

As usual, I turned to the Bonellis. In fact, they were about to leave for the country, so I told my stepmother that they were leaving in a couple of days, even though I knew they weren't leaving for ten, and I persuaded her to go with us to say good-bye.

Unfortunately, Signor Bonelli's office was closed, so our stepmother had to go up with us. This time, however, Maria was thinking of me, and she whispered as she shook my hand, "He went to Paris, to the Exposition." Then she turned to our stepmother and talked about other things, and I was left standing there, cold and pale, with a pain in my heart.

Paris! So it was possible, then, that people really went to Paris and came back? I stood there for a while speechless and paralyzed. Gradually, I came to my senses; my ears were buzzing, the way they do when you faint, and, in the midst of the buzz of general conversation, of which I didn't understand a single word, I burst out with the courage born of desperation, "The Exposition's in Paris, isn't it?"

My stepmother answered, "That's nothing new! People have been talking about it for a year now. . . ." And she went on with the conversation that I had interrupted, saying that "we didn't have a country house, because country houses are a passive investment, and when she bought land she would do so as an investment for her heir. . . ."

I interrupted again, asking anxiously, "Do a lot of people go there?"

"To the country?"

"No, to Paris."

"Well, I declare! She certainly has Paris on the brain! Are you hoping that I'll take you?"

"No, you know . . . I was just asking . . ."

Giuseppina said, "The Carotti have gone from Novara, and the Marchesa Fossati, and the Preatoni, and then a group of young men . . ."

She glanced at me to warn me that she was talking about him, but she was so discreet that she didn't mention his name or any name that might be associated with his; and she continued, "They'll be in Paris for a month, then they'll spend a month in London, then they'll visit other parts of England, as well as Belgium and Holland. . . ."

I exclaimed in dismay, "But they'll be gone forever!"

"Yes, for quite a while. It's an educational trip. But they're due back on All Saints' Day."

∞

As the Feast of All Saints drew nearer, I became calmer. I no longer thought of his absence, but of the joy of his return, of meeting him on the street, of seeing him in church.

On All Saints' Eve we went to the Bonellis'. This year, however, they had stopped their piano lessons, so they seldom saw the piano teacher, and they had no news of Mazzucchetti.

Then Giuseppina said, "They're certainly coming back today. I know that Crosio is returning this evening, and I believe that Mazzucchetti is, too."

Titina later observed that Giuseppina always seemed to know what Crosio was doing, and that "something must be going on." But I didn't care a fig about anyone else; I was completely absorbed in my own love.

On the morning of All Saints' Day, as I was dressing for mass, I said to my sister, "I'm afraid that I'll faint when I see him enter the church."

And she answered, "Don't get carried away. He probably won't come today. He just got back here, to spend All Saints' with his family; he won't want to leave his mother on his first day back."

During mass I kept turning around every time I heard the door close. I scandalized the faithful and got a good scolding from my aunt, but Onorato was not to be seen.

On the Day of the Dead I awoke convinced that some catastrophe had occurred; and I immediately remembered *my* catastrophe, and began to cry on Titina's shoulder, before I even got out of bed.

In the afternoon, while Titina, who was cooking that week, was preparing the bean soup that is eaten all over our province on the Day of the Dead, I felt my heart overflowing with bitterness, and my eyes with tears. I threw my work into the basket and stood by the window and watched the fine streams of rain pouring down, sobbing silently to myself.

All at once I saw Signor Bonelli come through the street door below, cross the courtyard as he looked up happily at our windows, and disappear into Papa's study.

My heart leapt. I had a presentiment that this unusual visit must regard me. Without daring to contemplate the hope that surged timidly inside me, I ran to Titina and whispered to her what I had seen.

Without losing her composure, she went on dicing the pork rind to cook with the "beans for the dead" into even cubes. She said, "It's clear that Mazzucchetti is back, and that he's sent Bonelli to propose marriage."

I threw my arms around her neck, buried my face on her shoulder, and broke into nervous sobs. She shrugged her shoulders without bitterness, but she was rather embarrassed. Staring fixedly down at the pork rind that she was chopping rapidly she said, "Are you crazy? Go upstairs to the bedroom. Listen, the boy's coming. Just imagine if he tells his mother that you're carrying on like this!" Then she added, heaving a loud sigh and looking down sadly at the cutting board, "I can't wait until you get married! We can't go on like this!"

I went up to my room in a very agitated state. Downstairs in the study the crucial question of my future was being settled. In the kitchen I heard Titina talking with our stepmother, who had gone in to help her, and laughing at the little boy, who was asking, "Why do dead people eat beans?"

Then Papa, who had apparently come to the kitchen door, called our stepmother: "Marianna! Come into the bedroom for a minute!"

As soon as I heard the door close behind her, I flew into the kitchen and asked my sister, "Titina, what did Papa look like? Was he happy?"

"Yes, he was rubbing his hands together."

From her bedroom our stepmother called twice in a loud voice: "Titina! Titina!"

My sister answered, "I'm coming!" And as she was untying her apron she whispered, "They want to ask me if it doesn't bother me too much if my little sister gets married first. Your fate is in my hands!"

And she went out, laughing.

They went on talking for some time, while I waited on pins and needles. I needed to unburden myself so much that I went behind the screen and told my aunt that perhaps Bonelli had come to relay a marriage proposal from a very rich, very nice young man, an only child. . . .

My aunt was very happy and urged me to let her come visit us in the country at least one month a year, saying, "Although you might not think so, the year passes very slowly behind this screen."

Loud footsteps were heard in the kitchen, and Papa said, "Denza, where are you?"

I came out from behind the screen, smiling at my aunt, who was nodding meaningfully at me, and followed my father to his room, where he held the door open for me.

I found my stepmother sitting by the fire, with Titina standing in front of her with eyes lowered; she was red in the face, as though she had been crying. Papa sat down on the other side of the fireplace, and I stood near my sister. Papa said, "Denza, my dear, your sister tells us that you're very depressed and that you couldn't live without her company, or at least that you would be quite unhappy. Is this true?"

I didn't understand at all. How on earth could my sister possibly think that I would miss her so much when I was married to Onorato? Of course I loved her, but I couldn't wait to get away; if I had anything to regret, it was that I wouldn't miss her enough.

In any event, I didn't want to give up my own happiness on account of my sister's affection for me. She was asking too great a sacrifice. I answered, "It all depends on whom I would be with in her absence. . . ."

My stepmother interrupted in obvious irritation, "Well! It does seem to me that your father's company, and that of the person who has been like a mother to you, should suffice!"

I looked at her in total bafflement. Was I going to live with them even after I got married? In that case, why wouldn't Titina be there, too? This was the question that I blurted out: "But where would Titina be?"

"How preposterous! With her husband!"

Titina let out a great sob and began to cry, covering her face with her hands. I exclaimed joyfully, "Oh! Is she getting married, too?"

My stepmother looked at me in astonishment, then said to my stepfather: "*Too!* You see, this young lady thought she was the one getting married. On the other hand, you're partly to blame, because you never make things clear." Then she turned to me and continued, "Here's the situation: we have received a proposal of marriage for your sister, but she hesitates to accept because she doesn't want to leave you; she says you're so depressed. . . . And why should you be, anyhow? It seems to me that nobody here is giving you any reason to be. . . ."

She embarked on a long discourse, but I was no longer listening. Her first words had given me such a shock that they left me cold and trembling, and I didn't answer.

Papa said to me sternly, "But Denza, don't you have anything at all to say to Titina, who is willing to sacrifice herself for you?"

I stammered out, "I don't want her to sacrifice herself. Of course she should get married! Anyhow, no one can do anything about my depression. . . . It will be the death of me! It surely will!"

And I ran out sobbing, while my stepmother told my father, "That girl needs looking after. . . . She's very high-strung. . . ."

∽

My sister's suitor was Antonio Ambrosoli, the son of the pharmacist in Borgomanero, the one who had been engaged to our cousin there for three years.

Just as the marriage contract was about to be signed, our cousin had refused to live with the groom's parents; he, for financial reasons, had not been able to leave them, and the long-hoped-for marriage had failed to come off.

This information terrified me. True, rather than give up Onorato, I would have resigned myself to living with his father, mother, and all of his relatives on both sides of his family, past and present, including his most distant cousins. But what if there were some other reason that his parents had opposed our marriage? And what if, like Antonio, he had simply given up?

Our stepmother, who didn't like things to drag on, decided that my sister's wedding would take place in a month. Thus the time was so taken up with preparations that I was quite distracted from my never-ending love problems.

When the great day came we had not yet finished preparing the trousseau. We didn't even go to bed the night before, and when dawn came that morning we were all already dressed in our best.

Because I had grown so much I had ended up having to let down my skirts whether I wanted to or not. For the occasion I had a new dress of bottle-green wool, which touched the ground, a little green felt hat, and a cape that matched my dress. And my sister, touched by my red hands, had told her husband-to-be to give me a muff of fake ermine as a gift.

How I longed to have Onorato see me dressed like that! And my hair was also parted low over my forehead! But nobody saw me, because the ceremony took place at six-thirty in the morning, without fanfare or guests, and we went directly from the church to the train station, to see the newlyweds off for Borgomanero.

With their departure, the house sank back into its usual gloom.

But Christmas was coming, and I consoled myself with the thought that Onorato would certainly come home to spend the holidays with his family. I repeated to myself a proverb alluding to some old legend that my aunt would repeat apropos of Christmas and people far away: "At Christmas everyone turns up, even bandits!"

Even though I wasn't usually particularly religious, that year I went out every morning at seven with my aunt, who was observing the nine days of Christmas at San Marco. I felt that the value of my devotion was multiplied by the early morning hour, those dark, deserted streets, and the ice from the night before that crackled underfoot.

In the dark church I would kneel in contrition and, staring with beseeching eyes at the faraway light of the candles on the altar, I would whisper fervently, "Oh, Jesus, let him come back! Oh, Jesus, let him come back!" And I would sing the litany and the *tantum ergo* so loudly that I became hoarse; but to me that mournful dirge and those incomprehensible Latin words all reiterated the same plea: "Oh, Jesus, let him come back!"

On December 22 the Bonellis came to tell us that Giuseppina was going to be married. Her father announced the news formally, and the bride-to-be blushed just a bit, not too much; she shook our hands energetically and said without skipping a beat, "He's a captain in the Guides. His father was a colonel, the famous Colonel Crosio who died at the Battle of Solferino. Carlo Alberto thought highly of him and considered him a friend. His mother comes from old Piedmontese nobility, and lives near Racconigi. Her small estate borders on the royal park, and when Carlo Alberto went hunting there he would occasionally stop at his colonel's modest villa . . ."

She said all this as though she were talking about some new man whom she had only known since he had asked for her hand, one of whom she knew only these generalities. She didn't say a word about their feelings, about how they had happened to fall in love and get engaged—and this must have happened sometime before because Titina had always noticed that the Bonellis were well informed concerning Crosio's every move.

The two of them did everything with propriety, and never made scenes, like well-bred people—everything, even when it came to love. I was so taken aback by her dignified reserve that I didn't dare ask about Onorato.

How bored I was that year with preparations for Christmas, which in our house began a week before the holiday!

Usually my sister and I would laugh and laugh as we got up on stoves and tables, on the chest, and even on the top of the fireplace, in order to crown the kitchen pots that hung on the walls with laurel leaves, "Just as they used to crown the poets on the Campidoglio," Papa would say. And while we were cooking, one of us would say to the other, "Get me down that big 'poet,' or the smaller one!"

While we were arranging the crèche for the little boy we had discovered that one of the Three Kings, the one bearing incense, looked like Onorato, and we called the kings the Three Musketeers.

That year, instead, I was sad and alone. As I was arranging the Musketeers at the back of the crèche I remembered that Titina had said the Christmas before, "Those blessed Musketeers are always standing at the door with their gifts, but they never come in." A year had passed, and my Musketeer was still standing at the door— if in fact he was still there at all. Since he was so far away, how could I know?

In January Giuseppina was married with great pomp, but I had to be content with mingling with the crowd in church along with my stepmother, with seeing the bride dressed in white and the groom in his dress uniform, and his mother as majestic as a queen, and all the ladies in dresses with trains who kept the crowd back, and the men in formal black attire, among whom was Papa, who held a big scroll in his hand. It contained an epithalamion that he was to read at the wedding breakfast, which Signor Bonelli had had printed at his own expense. Actually, Papa had found the epithalamion among his youthful poems, in the folder that he kept in the cabinet in his room along with the family mementos. But he had worked hard to adapt the wedding poem to the present circumstances, complaining that "the Muse no longer smiled at him as she used to." He talked about Hymen, then about the Madonna, and Saint Joseph, the bride's patron saint, because Papa "knew poetic language, but he didn't forget that he was a Christian."

In the spring I found out that Onorato was in Soleure and that he planned to remain there all year, in order to become more fluent in German.

These two weddings, so close together, had seemed to make my own all the more possible. Now suddenly, the idea of a whole year of separation, of an indefinite period of waiting, was a devastating blow. Nevertheless, I resigned myself and went on for twelve months more without losing faith.

Many things happened during that time, both pleasant and painful. My sister had a child. Giuseppina's husband was ordered to garrison in Palermo, and she went with him across the sea. My stepmother's son stopped wearing skirts, put on pants, and went to school. And my poor aunt came down with a rheumatic attack that was worse than the others, was sick for a month, and finally passed away as quietly as she had lived, into the next world in which she had such faith.

Papa had lit many a lamp to the Madonna during her illness; but this time his remedy did not work. And the kitchen seemed even larger and sadder now, without that screen.

Then soon after her death, Maria got married, too, and, after a short honeymoon, returned home with her husband to live in her father's house, so that he wouldn't be alone in his old age.

Of the four of us, I, the beauty, was the last to be married.

Finally, one evening in May, as we were strolling along the avenue, I saw Onorato with the two remaining Musketeers. As he passed near me, he looked at me just as though he had seen me the day before. I felt a wild surge of joy, and I thought: This is it! It's my turn now!

And every day I waited for his proposal.

But the proposal didn't come. Again, he began to look at me when we met and to come to church and stand at the head of our pew, his eyes fixed on me—those eyes that continued to affirm the unspoken vow between us, strengthening my faith; and, though they made me more and more impatient, they gave me nonetheless the strength to go on waiting.

And, in fact, I went on waiting for another five or six months, happy that he had returned, satisfied that my future was secure.

One day Maria, who no longer spoke to me of Onorato since her marriage, and who rarely came to see us, came to pick me up to take me to lunch at her house. This novel event caused me to guess that she had some good news to tell me; I thought of the proposal, and my heart was beating hard as I went out.

In fact, while we were waiting for Signor Bonelli and Maria's husband to return home for lunch, she asked, "And you, my beauty, aren't you thinking about getting married? It's high time, you know. You're six months older than I am."

I started to answer, "As soon as he proposes . . ."

She interrupted with a forced laugh, exclaiming, "Ah, Mazzucchetti's proposal! That proposal is your phantom ship!"

"My 'phantom ship?'"

"Yes, you wouldn't understand. It's an opera. It means a goal that you're always aiming for, but that you never reach. An illusion."

"Do you think it's an illusion?"

"I see that the years are going by, and that he never proposes. . . . If I were you, I'd give up."

I shrugged my shoulders in annoyance, and she went on, "That fatty keeps other suitors away."

"What suitors?" I protested. "If no one else is interested in me . . ."

"I don't think that's the case at all. Everybody knows you're in love with him. My husband heard it in a café."

"In a café!"

"Of course, my dear. You live apart from the world, and so you don't know that your fine gentleman is compromising you with his eternal staring, which leads to nothing."

I was a bit offended, without knowing why. The conversation struck me as brutal and pointless. Why was she talking like this now, rather than a few years before? I didn't answer, but my silence must have told her that I was hurt, because she came to my side, took my hands in hers, and said, "Don't get angry; I'm saying these things because I care for you. If either of us could help you, my husband or I . . . do think about it. Is there something we could do for you? We're going to the country soon. Do you want to come with us, and stay away all fall and try to forget him . . . ? What do you think?"

I reflected for a long while. I felt that there was a hidden meaning in her words that escaped me. Finally I said, "Why should I forget him? After waiting so long . . . !"

She looked at me with an air of compassion that I found infuriating and said nothing more. I continued, "Forget him! The only thing that could make me decide to forget him would be finding out that he will never marry me."

Maria bowed her head as though she were ashamed of having wronged me in some way and whispered without looking at me, "Just suppose that's the case."

I shook off her hands, which were still holding one of mine, and pushed her away; as I stood up and looked her in the eyes, I screamed hysterically, "Why? What reason do you have to say this? Why will he never marry me? Is there something the matter with me? Tell me . . ."

She shook her head and, with her eyes still lowered, she answered, "Not with you, my poor Denza!"

"So then he's the one you have doubts about? Why? Tell me: does he have another wife?"

This time she raised her eyes, looked at me sorrowfully, clasping her hands together as though to ask my pardon, and said softly, "He's marrying the Borani girl."

I echoed, "He's marrying the Borani girl!"

I felt myself turning cold, and I was shaking like a leaf and could say nothing more. I felt that every link that had bound me to life had suddenly broken, and that after such a cataclysm my life was over and there was nothing for me to do but die.

Maria was looking at me in dismay. I had fallen on the sofa; she knelt silently beside me. My chest heaved with sobs, and my throat ached. I held back for a minute, and then I abandoned myself in her arms—sobbing in despair, saying that I wanted to die, or become a nun, that I couldn't go out anymore, because everybody who saw me would laugh, and I would die of shame.

Maria waited patiently for me to give vent to my feelings, without contradicting me or trying to console me, until my deluge of tears was finished. Only then did she say, with great delicacy, that I had always attached too much importance to his ardent looks, that he had been shrewd and had been careful not to commit himself in any way; that of course he liked me, because I was beautiful, and if I had had Signorina Borani's dowry he would have preferred to marry me; but he was a selfish man, and he didn't have the courage to give up a dowry. And he wasn't worth crying over, and above all I must not give him the satisfaction of having made me his victim, of having upset me. I must appear indifferent. She understood how difficult and painful this was, but that was my heroic task. I must perform it in order to maintain my dignity. First I must compose myself, so that her father and husband, and later my family, wouldn't notice anything. . . . I was more moved by the last consideration than anything else. In truth, I could not go home and say, "The reason that I'm crying and upset and making scenes is that my beloved has abandoned me."

I washed my face with cool water and got through that lunch as best I could; both men had the courtesy to pretend that they knew nothing and that they didn't notice my altered appearance. That evening, when my stepmother, seeing my swollen eyes and how pale I was, looked at me aghast, I whispered, "We were talking about Auntie." And I went to my room and got undressed.

The next day there were the inevitable household chores, which helped me to overcome, if not my pain, at least its outward manifestations! Although I was sad and talked little, and was often on the verge of tears, I carried on, pretending that I was only grieving because I was still in mourning.

Thus I got through the most difficult and painful phase of the catastrophe. Later on I went with Maria to her country house, where I remained until after the wedding, that sort of elegant wedding that the wealthy have, which was too talked about in Novara for me to remain in town without enduring a great deal of pain and mortification.

On my return I resumed my normal life, and little by little I grew accustomed to the terrible idea of not being loved. When I happened to run into Onorato, he would look at me just as he had before. If it were not for his wife, I could have deluded myself that he was still in love with me and gone on hoping indefinitely. Maria told me, "It's better that he got married; otherwise he might have made you end up as an old maid like your aunt, living and dying behind a screen."

This idea terrified me, and I had to admit that it was indeed better this way. Thus encouraged, she went on in that vein of girlish mischievousness, which still cropped up from time to time: "If your papa finds out, he'll light a lamp to the Madonna in thanksgiving."

∽

After that milestone there was a long period, a very long one, during which absolutely nothing happened. A hard, tedious period filled with household tasks, insipid conversation, and routine occurrences: holidays, family parties, my little brother's exams and prizes, my stepmother's minor illnesses, visits to my sister, and hers to me. Nothing that affected me or left any impression, until the Carnival of 1875.

That year Giuseppina, who had fallen ill after a miscarriage, came to spend the winter in Novara, and her sister decided to give a musical soirée for her, followed by dancing later in the evening.

It was the first time that I'd had the opportunity to go to a party, and I spent a good deal of time thinking about what I would wear. We had received the invitation in the afternoon; the party was to take place two days later.

That evening at dinner I said, "I could wear my white dress from last summer . . ."

Papa merely pointed out that I might feel cold. But my stepmother objected, "Just as it is? All white? I think it's too youthful for a girl your age."

I think that at that moment the blood must have coursed through my veins three times faster than usual, because I felt a flash of heat mount to my head from my heart, which was beating so hard that it seemed to shake my entire body. But in spite of this instantaneous impression, I could not manage to think as quickly— how old I was or whether that dress was suitable—and I burst out, "My age! Am I an old lady, then, who can't wear white?"

And my stepmother answered, with her ruthless sincerity, "No, you're not an old lady, but you are a mature young woman."

Oh, what a blow that was! Not even Onorato's abandonment had been so devastating. A mature young woman! And it was true. I was over twenty-five! I had never thought about it before. Age had slowly crept up on me, imperceptibly, since I still led the same life I had led at fifteen, still subservient to my father and stepmother.

. . . Indeed, that child I used to carry about in my arms was now a little man of ten who went to secondary school.

That evening, as I sat with my legs dangling from my bed, blue with cold, I remained plunged in these sad thoughts for a long time. Over twenty-five, almost twenty-six. In four years I would be thirty! I remembered how my sister and cousins and I had laughed at a young woman of twenty-eight who put on girlish airs and didn't dare to go out by herself. Once when she said "when I get married" we made fun of her for days. Another time when she happened to say "girls like us" as we were talking, oh, what scenes we made! We thought this was the height of the ridiculous.

And now I was in the same boat. An old maid! I would no longer be able to talk about my marital prospects, because people would make fun of me behind my back. Other girls considered me old. And they were right! My contemporaries, even Maria, who was younger than I was, were married; they had school-age children; they were women. My life was over. I saw my poor aunt's screen rise up menacingly before me, and I shed silent tears of despair, which flowed from my cheeks onto my nightshirt, without noticing that my legs were freezing and that my whole body was cold as ice. An old maid!

The next morning I had a bad cold, which gave me an excuse, along with the fact that I didn't know how to dance, not to go to Maria's party. The prospect of appearing for the first time in society as a mature young woman, someone who was too old to wear white, was too humiliating and painful.

The next six months, from that unforgettably sad day until the following August, were the most miserable of my life.

∞

In August that same year, one evening when I had gone to bed early, I woke up very thirsty around eleven and went into the kitchen barefoot in the dark to get some water.

The heat was suffocating, so all the doors were open, and I could hear Papa and my stepmother talking in their room. Papa was saying, "I don't even dare suggest him to her. A girl who's young and beautiful . . ."

My stepmother answered, "Of course she's beautiful, and she's in her prime. But she's getting a bit old to be a bride."

"What? How old is she? Twenty-two or -three . . . ?"

Poor Papa, *he* didn't think that I was an old maid! To him I was still the girl that he had shepherded along the main roads while he recited the *Iliad*.

My stepmother corrected him. "She's twenty-six. As I said, she's young. But there are so many girls of eighteen or twenty who are just as beautiful, and rich besides; so naturally, having no dowry and being a little older, she mustn't be too particular if she wants to get married. After all, he's the first one who's come along. . . ."

I tiptoed quickly back to bed, with my heart beating violently. In fact, he *was* the first one who'd come along. Who was he? Whoever he was, I was very lucky that he had.

I was prepared to accept him; the very fact that he was interested in me was in his favor. *He* didn't think I was too old! I only hoped that Papa wouldn't decide to be more particular than I was! Why didn't he dare to propose him to me? Could he be old? Oh, Lord! How many different scenarios and love stories I concocted that night!

It was my stepmother who announced, the next day after lunch, "Listen, Denza, we have a possible match for you, but it's not a brilliant one."

Papa was there, but he was reading the newspaper, as though to say that he wanted nothing to do with this proposal. I asked very nervously, "Who is he?"

"A notary from Vercelli, who's coming to practice in Novara."

Up until now, I didn't suspect that there was anything wrong, but evidently something was. I went on asking questions: "Is he old?"

"No, he's forty." I was about to say that forty seemed old to me. But I remembered that I was old, so I said instead, trying to find out what could be wrong apart from age, "Is he very poor?"

"On the contrary, he's quite well off. And he'll be a partner in Notary Ronchetti's practice, when he comes to Novara."

What could be wrong with him? Of course: his looks. I asked, with great trepidation, "So he's hideous, then?"

"Hideous, no . . . but he does have one defect. . . ."

I could hardly breathe. I didn't dare ask what it could be. My stepmother let me get used to the idea of a defect, or perhaps some deformity, so that it would be less of a blow, then she went on, "He has a growth, you know, a rather large wart, here on his right temple."

This upset me. I had no idea how big a wart could get. Once in Borgomanero I had seen a peasant with a growth on his nose that was twice as big as the nose itself: a terrible sight. But this must be different. The other wasn't a wart; it must have been some terrible disease. . . . Finally I got up my courage and asked, "Is it very large?"

"No, of course not! It's the size of a walnut. If he combs his hair down low over his temples, it's hardly noticeable. . . ."

The idea of his combing his hair down and plastering it over this deformity in order to hide it bothered me even more than the wart itself. I thought it would be better if he could carry it off casually.

My stepmother went on, "In any event it won't hurt to see him. Before you refuse him, meet him."

I bowed my head in resignation. I didn't mind meeting him; on the contrary, I wanted to. What I did mind was how different marriage seemed now from what I had imagined.

It was Signor Bonelli who had proposed Notary Scalchi as a possible husband for me, just as he had proposed Antonio Ambrosoli for my sister several years before. It seemed that this distant cousin's mission in life was to find husbands for us. Thus it was, to my extreme embarrassment, at his house and in Maria's presence that I was to meet my suitor.

We went over to the Bonellis' after their dinner, at about seven. The prospective groom had not yet arrived. They were openly discussing the meeting and the circumstances that had led up to it.

Maria was saying, "He's a handsome man; he only has a few faults. Besides, he's already rejected some potential brides with dowries, you know. Signorina Vivanti was suggested to him, but he refused her because she was too short. He was introduced to her when she was sitting on a rather high sofa, and he saw that her feet didn't touch the floor. . . ."

Signorina Vivanti was a horrid little thing whose relatives and friends had been trying unsuccessfully to marry her off for several years. What sort of man could he be, to be offered such a bride?

He arrived almost immediately after that, and my first impression was not unfavorable. He was tall and rather big, but well proportioned. He had a crop of light brown hair that stood straight up on his head. It was clear that he didn't even try to comb it down over his temples in order to hide his flaw. Moreover, it wouldn't even have been possible, because his hair was so bristly that it was unmanageable.

His first impression must also have been favorable, for as soon as he had located me and looked at me for a moment, he turned as red as an adolescent, and lost the nonchalant air that he had had when he had entered. When he was introduced to me, he was momentarily nervous, and he blushed again when he caught me looking at his right temple.

But he regained his composure immediately, and joined in the conversation that the men were having. He had a pleasant voice, and he was well spoken. He talked about the rice fields in Vercelli, deploring the fact that they were so close to the city; however, he termed the concern of writers for the rice workers exaggerated and overly sentimental. He said that, if humanely treated by their employers, it was possible for them to do this work without suffering any ill effects. Then he outlined a whole system of hygiene for these peasants that I found extremely boring. I would have preferred that he talk to me of his hopes, of the impression I had made on him . . . in short, of love.

Maria, like a diligent household mistress, managed to arrange for us to be alone. She had us all go out on the balcony; then a short while later, she went in with my stepmother to make tea, and the others followed. We were left alone on the balcony.

I kept my eyes fixed on the street below and remained silent, eager to hear what he would say. He seemed to reflect at length, because he said nothing for a while, then leaned on the railing beside me and said, "Signorina, I haven't heard your opinion on the matter that we were just discussing."

I thought that he might have discussed our marriage with Papa or Signor Bonelli. I felt a blush suffuse my face, and I asked in embarrassment, "What matter?"

"The rice fields."

I thought he must be joking, and I looked at him in astonishment. He continued, however, without noticing, "My money—what little I have, because I'm not a large landowner—is invested in rice fields. And I live there for part of the year in order to supervise the work myself. This is an obligation of conscience for owners of rice fields; otherwise, they have to leave everything to foremen, and in that case it's true that our poor day laborers are subjected to exhausting work, and that they are poorly paid, underfed and miserably housed, and treated like slaves."

I answered in some irritation, "I don't know anything about it, you know. We have a little land near Gozzano, woods and vineyards. I'm not familiar with rice fields."

"But you might find yourself in the position of having to know something about them, or of owning them. And I want you to know how necessary it is to sacrifice oneself in order to oversee them personally. I say 'sacrifice oneself' because I understand that it really is a sacrifice, especially for a lady. For example, my house is very large, comfortable, and even quite elegant; but it's not a country house where you can have guests and have a good time. You can take walks all day long, but at night you have to go to bed early and stay shut up in the house by the fire."

I understood that he wanted to prepare me for the life that awaited me, but I would have liked him to put a bit more feeling into what he was saying. I was discouraged. Perhaps he noticed, because he said, "I'm used to it, and I'm glad to do it because of my feelings of humanity; but I feel that if I had someone near me, during those months, those long, foggy evenings . . ."

He hesitated for a moment, then paused; perhaps he was seeking some sign of encouragement in my eyes to elaborate on that *someone;* but I did not dare turn around, and he concluded with a very mysterious little laugh that "I would grow even more used to it."

Maria came out with two cups of tea, and as she handed me mine, she whispered, "How's it going?" And seeing that I was blushing and embarrassed, she concluded on her own that things were going well.

I was quite discouraged, because I saw my romantic dreams vanishing before the reality of this man, into the mists of his rice fields. However, I was determined to marry him so that I wouldn't be an old maid.

Everyone came out on the balcony sipping tea from their cups, convinced that those few minutes had been sufficient for us to decide our whole lives.

In fact, they had been. We had made up our minds.

Signor Scalchi left before we did, and Signor Bonelli, who had seen him to the door, came back in looking very satisfied, saying, "He's happy, and he claims that he couldn't possibly hope for a more beautiful bride, or a nicer one. He's really in love, and the only thing he's afraid of is being rejected. His voice was trembling as he spoke to me. He was on the verge of tears when we were shaking hands: I was quite moved."

I was thunderstruck at this depth of emotion that had showed itself only as he was about to leave, while with me it had not prompted a single word. Nonetheless, I was pleased and flattered. This might also help me feel more at ease. Everyone was looking at me, waiting for my answer; noticing my silence, my stepmother asked, "And what do you have to say? Do you like him or not?"

I stammered out: "If only he didn't have that wart . . ."

"Ah! Of course it would be better if he didn't. But he does; it's a fact. You have to accept him as he is or refuse him."

I came up with another objection, in order to save my dignity. "Couldn't he have it taken off?"

There was a moment of embarrassed silence. Everyone was looking at me, and I seemed to see an expression of disapproval on every face. Then Signor Bonelli answered, "How can we possibly ask him to do such a thing? What's more, if an operation were possible, he would have had it when he was younger. . . ."

My stepmother said sternly, "I declare! Endangering a man's life for a whim . . ."

And Maria pointed out, "It would be quite mortifying for him to hear that you hold his defect against him, now that he's met you and fallen in love. . . . Be generous; accept him as he is. . . ."

Papa interrupted her. "Don't try to influence her, Maria. Let her think about it. Let her pray to God for guidance; let her also light a lamp to the Madonna, and then do whatever her heart tells her to do. This is a matter of her entire life. If she doesn't want him for a husband it's better for her to say no right away, so that she doesn't have regrets later."

I wasn't the least inclined to say no. I bowed my head in silence; but everyone understood that I would accept him, and for the rest of the evening they talked about Scalchi's fortune, his land in Borgo Vercelli, his office in Novara, and his associate, as though they were things that were of great personal interest.

The next day I gave my definitive consent.

The groom was welcomed into our house. He brought me the usual wedding presents, found a house, and had his furniture from Vercelli moved there; and finally the day was set for the wedding, which, thanks to the groom's financial means, was to be formal.

∽

From that time on, I no longer had time to think about my past aspirations; I barely even had time to think about my fiancé. The wedding, with its advance preparations, required all my attention, as well as the rest of the family's. My sister left her son in the care of her mother-in-law and came to Novara to help us. We were out the whole day shopping or making calls. And in the evening my sister and I copied out in our best penmanship an epithalamion that Papa had composed for my wedding.

As soon as one copy was done, he would correct it—there was always something to correct in our copies—then roll it up, tie it with a red ribbon, and write the name of the recipients on it with notarylike precision: "Signor Agapito Bonelli, Engineer; and daughter and son-in-law, Signor and Signora Crespi." "Signor Martino Bellotti, Doctor of Medicine, Surgery, and Obstetrics; and spouse."

In the meantime my stepmother was planning the wedding breakfast and the guest list, and she would interrupt from time to time to consult with us at great length. As far back as I could remember we had never invited anyone to lunch at our house. We usually ate in the kitchen at one o'clock, and when Uncle Remigio or one of the Ambrosoli or some other out-of-town relative turned up he was offered whatever we were eating, nothing more, at that kitchen table wedged between the burners and my aunt's screen.

Now the screen was no longer there, but in any event it wasn't possible to have a wedding breakfast in the kitchen. We would have to have it in the living room.

This unusual situation threw us into a tizzy. The sacks of corn, potatoes, chestnuts, and everything else would have to be taken away; the covers would have to come off the furniture, curtains would have to be hung, and the round tables would have to be removed so that we could bring in the big kitchen table instead. Then that wasn't long enough, so we brought the two rather low round tables back in and put one at each end, which looked strange and not at all attractive. None of our tablecloths were the right size for this elongated table. So the two round tables were covered with separate cloths, so that they formed separate entities one step down from the central table.

Papa suggested that we hide this discrepancy beneath a layer of flowers, but he decided not to sit there at the head of the table, as had first been planned, because since he would be lower down he would not dominate the assembled guests when he read the epithalamion. He decided to sit at the center of the main table with my stepmother facing him, even though this new French vogue wasn't to their liking. My wedding dress was also the subject of great discussion. Although the wedding was to be quite formal, it wasn't really formal enough for a white dress. I had counted on wearing a colored silk dress with a train, which I was quite proud of, but Maria thought it inappropriate for the occasion and "provincial." Then my stepmother had the idea that I should wear a travel outfit and, although it was pointed out to her that we weren't going anywhere, she stood firm and the travel outfit won out.

The long-awaited, long-feared day finally arrived. When I was all dressed up like a *touriste* about to take a trip around the world, I began to cry, hugging everybody before we went off to church just as though we would never see each other again in this life. I cried so much during the ceremony that it was a miracle if anyone heard me say "I do," which I tried to utter between a couple of sobs. Then I went on crying quietly all during the breakfast, answering with a little sob every time that anyone paid me a compliment, until they stopped paying them, and everyone ate quietly, talking about serious things—about the crops that were very good that year, about "our wines" of the upper Novarese that are in no way inferior to those of Piedmont, and about the second wine of the harvest, "the so-called *vinello* that is excellent, and so appropriate for family use."

Then during the fruit course, when Papa unfurled one of the many sheets that I had personally written out and began to read aloud—

On this day sacred to Hymen, I pray
the Virgin and saints who are propitious to you—

those verses, which I knew by heart, moved me so that I broke into a flood of tears, and they had to take me out of the room.

∞

And so I was married after all those years of love, of poetry and romantic dreams.

Now I have three children. Papa, who had himself lit the lamp that he advised me to light on the day that we met Scalchi, says that the Madonna guided me. And my stepmother claims that I've gotten back that blooming, rustic look that I used to have when I was younger.

The truth is that I'm putting on weight.

Un matrimonio in provincia, a short novel written by Maria Antonietta Torriani-Torelli in 1885, is a small masterpiece of modern Italian literature. As her nom de plume implies, the Marchesa Colombi wrote for an upper-class female public; she was one of a number of women writers who catered to this sizable market in late-nineteenth-century Italy. She was a fascinating cultural figure who absorbed the prevailing literary currents of her time and, in this novel at least, transcended them.

She was born Maria Antonietta Torriani in Novara in 1840—she coquettishly claimed in 1846—and died in 1920. Her family seems to have resembled Denza's in the novel (in real life, however, it was Torriani's mother who remarried, so that Maria Antonietta acquired an elderly stepfather instead of a stepmother).[1] She left Novara at thirty and moved to Milan, where she became a journalist as well as a novelist and an all-around *femme de lettres*. Her projects ran the gamut from translating from the French to writing the lyrics to a melodrama called *The Violin of Cremona* that was presented at La Scala in 1882. She was also an active feminist who taught English in a Milanese *liceo* founded to offer women an alternative education. She was married briefly to Eugenio Torelli-Viollier, the founder of the famous *Corriere della sera*. Her marriage gave her entrée to Milanese literary circles in the years when the literary movement called *verismo* (Italian realism) was at its height and where the influence of French and other European literatures was inescapable.

Though most of her other novels, such as *In risaia* and *Prima morire*, are interesting in terms of literary and social themes, they are not exceptional as works of literature. Even in Italy, her work is not well known. Without the intervention of two of the great Italian writers of the twentieth century, Italo Calvino and Natalia Ginzburg, *A Small-Town Marriage* might well have been doomed to the oblivion that often awaits the work of so-called popular novelists. Long out of print, this novella was chosen by Calvino to be part of an Einaudi series, *Le centopagine* (*Works of a Hundred Pages*), and was reprinted in 1973. It was recommended to him by Natalia Ginzburg, who wrote in her preface to the new edition of the tremendous impact that this novel had had on her as a young girl, implying that it had influenced her own idea of what literature should be.

Ginzburg writes in her introduction to the 1973 edition: "What I found unusual in *Un matrimonio in provincia* was a way of presenting people and facts without romanticizing or idealizing them, in a straightforward, light and nonchalant way that I wasn't accustomed to in books, because the books that I was used to reading overflowed with cloying sentimentality."[2] Although the Marchesa Colombi was not the only late-nineteenth-century writer to portray women whose romantic impulses were defeated by middle-class society—Mathilde Serao and Neera did also—what distinguishes her, as Italo Calvino points out, is her concrete, down-to-earth prose and the subtle underlying irony in which she couches this theme, "that self-reflexive irony that is the essence of humor."[3]

In a prolix era, the Marchesa Colombi wrote a spare novel that remains immensely appealing to modern tastes. One has only to compare it to Sibilla Aleramo's *Una donna* (*A Woman*), published twenty-one years later, in 1906, and widely regarded as the first "feminist" novel in Italy, to appreciate its originality. Although the two are very different, they do have in common the theme of a woman oppressed by the mores of provincial society as well as a first-person narrator. Aleramo's book, however, is never free of psychologizing and verbose self-analysis: it is an autobiography in the guise of a novel, whose chief interest for the reader of today is its revolutionary subject matter rather than its style. *A Small-Town Marriage*, on the other hand, not only shows a mature stylist at work: it is a work in which style and content are so seamlessly blended as to be one.

The story is told in the first person by Denza Dellara, the daughter of a provincial notary, who looks back on her sad childhood and adolescence from her vantage point as a married woman, the mother of three. Despite the title, however, the novel is not about her actual marriage, of which we know little until the last page; rather, it is about her expectations of marriage and how they sustain her during her dreary provincial youth, only to be ultimately dashed by economic reality. Romance is a flight from small-town reality, but this is no stereotypical rehashing of *Madame Bovary*. Denza's "Prince Charming," Onorato, is rich but grossly fat; Denza falls in love with him for no other reason but the fact that she is emotionally starved and he appears to admire her. She waits for him for years, although it is clear to all, including the reader, that he will never marry her because she has no dowry. Finally, when he marries another, she abandons her romantic dreams and settles for a well-to-do notary who is older than she is, in order to avoid the stigma of spinsterhood.

The story itself is simple; the problem is one of interpretation, of teasing out the truth that the author seeks to convey from Denza's first-person recounting of her romantic woes. It is no wonder that some critics, such as Giuliana Morandini, have chosen to interpret this more or less at its face value, as an early feminist portrayal of the evils of marriage, with its irony directed against the "conjugal bond."[4] Although it was written at around the same time, this is far from the territory covered, say, by Charlotte Perkins Gilman in "The Yellow Wallpaper." The Marchesa weaves a singularly complex narrative, in which nothing is as simple as it seems. Lucienne Kroha points out in her essay "The Marchesa Colombi's *Un matrimonio in provincia:* Style as Subversion" that *"behind the story told there lurks a story not told, a sub-text continuously suggested which the reader herself supplies and sees subverted at the same time"* (emphasis added).[5] The result is a sort of "antiliterary novel" which, "by virtue of its totally irreverent style and imagery, constantly challenges literature's depiction of reality."[6]

As Kroha states by way of response to those critics who see this as a feminist tract against marriage, it would be a mistake to read this only as a novel about gender politics. *A Small-Town Marriage* does not attack bourgeois institutions directly but instead deliberately plays with established literary conventions and their implications. She suggests that the Marchesa finally finds her distinctive voice in this work by in fact rewriting the late-nineteenth-century Romantic bourgeois novel according to the new conventions of *verismo.*[7] However, by "realism" the Marchesa did not mean the conventional sort that prevailed in nineteenth-century literature (one might say the male school of realism). She deplored what she termed the "lack of reality" in the literature of her time, by which she meant that "entire area of human experience—the banal, the *quotidiano,* the nonexceptional—that has been largely excluded from literature, which, as a result, promotes a falsely romantic view of life in all its aspects."[8] As Torriani herself wrote, she is in favor of a literature that reflects "a way of considering life that makes it poetic without removing it from the practical sphere to the realm of the ideal."[9] In another novel she wrote that she wanted to convey "the prose of every-day life."[10] For example, readers familiar with Balzac cannot fail to note how the opening description of the bleak Dellara house, which foreshadows the emotional deprivation of its occupants and prepares us for Denza's romantic rebellion, recalls the famous description of the Maison Vauquer and its inhabitants at the beginning of *Le Père Goriot*, written fifty years before. However, the Marchesa dwells on everyday objects such as dead plants and prayer candles; the effect is much lighter, more playful and domestic than Balzac's dark gallery of the grotesque inhabitants of the underbelly of Parisian society.

How does all this relate to what Kroha tantalizingly terms the Marchesa's "subversive style"? In brief, Kroha points out that the story is told without the slightest sentimentalism; its irony is created by the "constant, implicit juxtaposition of the 'sublime' and the 'ridiculous,' the sublime being Denza's expectations of reality and the ridiculous being the intrusion of reality itself."[11]

This juxtaposition is achieved by the tension between the first-person narration, in which Denza tells her story with the naïveté of the young girl that she was, without reference to her present circumstances, and the reader's corrections of the narrator's recounting of events.[12] To give only one example, the reader knows from the time that Denza notices Onorato's change in demeanor during their meeting at the Café Cavour that economic reality has intruded and that his family will not let him marry the dowryless Denza. The narrator, however, is only momentarily daunted by the occurrence and continues her romantic vigil.

Yet the kinds of texts that are "subverted" in *A Small-Town Marriage* include not only the Romantic novel, as Kroha points out, but also those of opera and fairytales. First, opera: Denza is first seen by Onorato at a performance of *Faust*, although she does not see him because she is busy looking at herself in a mirror. She begins to identify with the character of Marguerite, who is also poor and burdened with the care of a child and household chores much as she herself is (being ignorant, however, she is unaware of Faust's metamorphosis or of his link with the devil, which slyly forecasts the instability of Onorato's "love"). Later, Onorato's declaration of love takes the form of a letter containing the aria "Un dì felice" from *La traviata:* the long-awaited letter arrives on Saw Day—a local custom during Lent in which suitors pursue the women whom they have admired at the balls during Carnival—only to be tossed in a pool of cabbage water by Denza's watchful stepmother (the accompanying turquoise saw ends up stuck to a piece of meat)!

Torriani pokes fun throughout at the familiar *topoi* of popular storytelling, particularly in the character of Denza's beloved, who is a delightful twist on the traditional Italian *principe azzurro,* or Prince Charming. Far from being handsome, he is enormously fat: the disappointed Denza describes him as a "sort of gray elephant" the first time she sees him. Onorato sees himself, quite unselfconsciously, as a very romantic figure. The first, and only, time that they actually meet and talk he confides his "secrets" to her: he and his friends are the Four Musketeers, who meet in a rented room where they put on fezzes and smoke and talk; he is a tragic figure, doomed to make the woman he loves unhappy, because an old crone once told him so during a storm! In fact, this fantastic prediction ironically proves true, but only because Denza clings to her romantic illusions for years, refusing to open her eyes to the realities of provincial society and human character.

In fact, the entire narrative is a sort of ironic fairytale, populated with characters like that of the wicked stepmother, who then reveal themselves to be something more than the cartoons they seem at first. Let us consider the stepmother, who suddenly enters and commands the affections of Denza's father, already hard put to "mother" his two adolescent daughters. Although her no-nonsense attitude at first seems cruel, as when she curtails her stepdaughters' evening walks in town ("the only time when we had ever seen any civilized, well-dressed people") and asks them not to come into the living room when she receives guests, she in fact is most often the person who merely speaks the truth. It is she who represents reality in the novel, both economic and social: it is she who transforms the bare living room with its meticulously arranged furniture, emblematic of the emotional deprivation of its occupants, into a sort of granary or storage room. She represents bourgeois, small-town reality, the truth of dowries and property and marriageable ages that Denza would like to ignore. Although we may dislike her and wish, as Denza does, that she could learn "a bit of kindness," she is far from wicked.

Denza herself is a sort of Cinderella figure, though one with comically large feet. She is condemned to wear clothes that are too small for her ample proportions because as the younger sister she must not eclipse her elder sister and thus ruin the latter's matrimonial prospects. Though the family is far from poor, she and her sister are expected to run the household, and Denza's special province is caring for her little half brother, born to Denza's father and stepmother, whom she refers to as the "brat." The descriptions of her wardrobe are hilarious, especially on the day when she is to go out walking in order to see Onorato for the first time. When she attempts to let down the flounce of a dress so as to cover her ankles, she unwittingly exposes her underwear to view and has to remedy the situation while the others wait. Though not precisely the victim of cruelty, she is the victim of middle-class indifference, propriety, and avarice, and there is no fairy godmother to relieve her distress: only Signor Bonelli, who eventually brings a proposal of marriage from Signor Scalchi.

Signor Scalchi, who turns up only at the very end of the book, is perhaps the most enigmatic figure in the novel. It is he who finally puts a merciful end to Denza's years of dreaming. She accepts his offer in order to escape the fate of her late aunt, her father's maiden sister, whose passive life, characterized by religious devotion and hypochondria, has been lived out behind a screen in the kitchen until her merciful death just before the novel's dénouement. Scalchi's fatal "flaw," which is probably the only reason he is available, is a large wart on his forehead. He seems to be a sort of Frog Prince; that is, he would be a prince if it were not for his deformity. Although a wart does not strike the reader as a worse defect than Onorato's obesity, which Denza had gladly put up with, the narrator describes him critically as a fate only slightly better than spinsterhood. She is puzzled by what she interprets as his coldness at their first meeting, when he wants to know how she would react to the lonely life that she would lead as the wife of an owner of rice fields who actually supervises them himself. He is, in fact, offering her his heart in a very decent way, but Denza is too caught up in her hunger for love to discern this, although she does understand that "he wanted to prepare me for the life ·that awaited me." She does not seem to react much to Scalchi personally at all; what she does mind, she says, is "how different marriage seemed now from what I had imagined."

"From what I had imagined" are in fact the key words. Scalchi is, in fact, marriage demystified: he does not talk to her of old women's prophesies, or send her operatic arias; he merely wants to know if she thinks she could be happy living the kind of life he can offer her. The brief scene on Maria's balcony in which this conversation takes place is very different from the parallel scene several years before on the balcony at Maria's country house, in which Denza first meets Onorato and he declares his love. Reality is not easy for Denza to swallow: she says of Scalchi, "I saw my romantic dreams vanishing before the reality of this man, into the mists of his rice fields."

Although Denza may not think much of Scalchi (in fact, after this "interview" with her suitor decides her fate, he vanishes from the book, to be obscured by wedding preparations, and Denza's

feelings toward him resurface only at the wedding, in the form of a flood of tears), it is evident in this scene that the Marchesa Colombi has given him at least a halfhearted blessing. Although he is an owner of rice fields who ironically expresses views somewhat different from the author's own, he is not one of those exploitative, absentee landlords that she criticized in her naturalistic novel of 1878, *In risaia*. Scalchi, in the general conversation that precedes the "unromantic" balcony scene with Denza, "talked about the rice fields in Vercelli, deploring the fact that they were so close to the city; however, he termed the concern of writers for the rice workers exaggerated and overly sentimental. He said that, if humanely treated by their employers, it was possible for them to do this work without suffering any ill effects. Then he outlined a whole system of hygiene for these peasants that I found extremely boring." While Denza cannot appreciate Scalchi's social conscience—his feelings for the rice workers are in fact the only instance of any awareness of or regard for the working classes in the book—the author nevertheless seems to. Scalchi is at the very least the moral superior of Onorato Mazzucchetti, who spends his time pretending to be one of Dumas's characters, learning German on the Grand Tour, and trying unsuccessfully to lose weight at the nineteenth-century equivalent of "fat farms."

It is perhaps Italo Calvino who should have the last word with respect to what sets this novel apart from others of its time and still makes it so readable today. Though he says that the Marchesa Colombi belongs to the late-nineteenth-century tradition of writers who evoke the silent dramas of emotionally frustrated women confined within the home, she is also something quite different "because when she depicts mean, cramped lives, boredom and dreariness, she presents her characters with a ruthless eye, precise strokes and grotesque deformity, so as to convey the greatest sadness with the lightest poetic touch."[13]

Notes

1. Pierobon, Ermenegilda, "L'enormità del reale: Una lettura di *Un matrimonio in provincia* della Marchesa Colombi," *Forum italicum* 30, no. 2 (1996): 296.

2. Critical notes in *Un matrimonio in provincia* (Novara: Centro Novarese di Studi Letterari, 1993), 107.

3. Ibid.

4. Giuliana Morandini, *La voce che è in lei: antologia della narrativa femminile italiaana tra '800 e '900* (Milan: Bompiani, 1980), 16.

5. Lucienne Kroha, "The Marchesa Colombi's *Un matrimonio in provincia:* Style as Subversion," in *Donna: Women in Italian Culture,* ed. Ada Testaferri (Ottawa: Dovehouse Editions, 1989), 162.

6. Ibid.

7. Ibid., 154.

8. Ibid., 158.

9. "Un 'avventura di un giornalistista," in *Dopo il caffè* (Bologna: Zanichelli, 1880), 218; Kroha, "The Marchesa Colombi's *Un matrimonio in provincia,*" 158. My translation.

10. *Prima morire* (Milan: Galli, 1896), 113, as quoted by Kroha, "The Marchesa Colombi's *Un matrimonio in provincia,*" 158. My translation.

11. Kroha, "The Marchesa Colombi's *Un matrimonio in provincia,*" 162.

12. Ibid.

13. Critical notes in *Un matrimonio in provincia,* 107.